Fragmented Love

His Warriors Book 6

By

Ronna M. Bacon

Psalm 136:26 Give thanks to the God of heaven, for his steadfast love endures forever.

Table of Contents

Chapter 1

Pulling his cap down further on his face to shade it from the early morning light, Jonah Bronson looked around. He sighed. He really didn't want to be here, at the local farmer's market, just like he was every Saturday. He really needed to be on his farm, working around his fields, harvesting the produce that needed it. His eyes searched the familiar faces he saw every week. Then, he frowned. The woman at the table next to him was new. He hadn't seen her there before. She didn't have any produce or what would normally be sold at the market. Instead, she was laying out brochures and plates of food.

He shrugged, not really interested in what she was doing. He spoke to the man on the other side of him, a local beekeeper, who worked closely with the local health food store to provide his honey and honey products. Jonah had known him all his life.

He turned once more to his own produce, studying the way he had laid it out. The same layout every week, just different produce, depending on the season. He sighed again. He was bored, and knew it. Lord, I'm here, but I really don't want to be. Why? I feel a restlessness in me I've never felt before. But why?

He turned once more as he heard a silvery, musical laugh from beside him. His aunt was talking to the woman next to him, then pointing at Jonah.

"Jonah, get yourself over here." His Aunt Lois wouldn't take no for an answer, he knew.

He reluctantly moved over to stand beside her, dropping a kiss on her cheek as he did so.

"Jonah, have you met Candace yet? She's new to town."

Jonah turned, expecting to see someone close to his aunt's age, but was surprised as he saw she was close to his. Red hair and grey eyes. What a combination, he thought.

"Hi." Her voice was soft. "I'm Candace Owens."

"Jonah Bronson. Nice to meet you." He picked up one of her brochures and scanned it. "You provide meals to shut ins, etc.?"

"I do. I used to work for a big company as a dietician but decided to branch out on my own. This seemed like a good fit." She studied him, taking in the black hair and green eyes. "I see you have produce for sale. Do you just sell here or can anyone buy from you?"

He shrugged. "I sell to local stores and restaurants." He paused, then turned back to his table, where he saw customers lining up. He handed over a business card. "Here. Call me at some point and we can discuss this further. I'm not sure how I can help you out, though."

She pocketed the card, her eyes thoughtful as she watched him move back to his table. His black hair and green eyes were a combination she didn't see much.

His aunt spoke. "Don't mind him, Candace. He's usually very focused when he's here. Although lately, I just don't know with him." She sighed and then moved to Jonah's table, waiting to speak with him.

Candace shook her head. Here I am, Lord. You directed me to this town, helped me to set up a business I enjoy, and now when I find a supplier, he's not real friendly. Now what?

Candace stood beside her car at the end of the morning, a sadness wafting through her body. Here she was in a new town, no friends, and feeling very lonely and low. She started to turn as she heard footsteps approaching her.

Shoved violently against her car, she struggled to get away from the arm holding her there. She couldn't see her assailant but could feel his breath on the back of her neck.

"Leave town, lady, and don't come back. We don't need the likes of you here."

A sudden shout had her assailant shoving her violently to the ground before she heard his running footsteps. Her eyes sank closed as she tried to regain her breath. She felt a hand on her arm and jerked away.

Jonah stood up for a moment and stared in the direction the man had run. A vague thought crossed his mind that he knew the man, but then he shrugged, crouching down once more beside Candace.

"Are you okay, Candace?" He kept his voice gentle as he spoke to her, his hand going out to help her sit up.

She nodded, her eyes finally flickering open to stare at him. "I think so." She leaned back against the tire. "Where'd he go?"

"He disappeared when I came up. Do you know who he was?"

She shook her head, then regretted it. "I don't think, I do. Some welcome to your town, mister."

Jonah gave a half smile, then stood as a patrol officer and the EMS squad approached. This was definitely not how he planned to end his morning.

❦ ❦ ❦ ❦

Candace looked around her small house, feeling something off, but not sure what it was. Someone had been in it, she was sure. She walked through, her eyes searching until she reached her office, then froze. She could see the paperwork on her desk dumped on the floor, her filing cabinet's lock broken and files all over the floor. She sighed, then reached for her phone. What next, she thought? She really didn't need this, she thought, as she reached for her phone. Her hand froze for a moment. What was the connection between this and what happened at the farmer's market? Had she really made the right choice to move to Elmton?

The patrol officer walked through her house and then paused beside her as she stood in the office doorway.

"Is anything missing?"

"I can't see that there is, but I'll have to sort all the paperwork back into proper files to see if there is. Who would do this?"

The officer shook his head. "It's pretty personal, I would think, doing this. Whoever it was wanted something. Let us know if there's anything more we can do."

Chapter 2

$\mathcal{J}$onah stood the next morning in the entry of the church, talking with friends, his eyes roving across the people gathered there prior to the service. He watched with interest as Candace entered, hesitation in her movements. He frowned as she moved through the crowd, largely ignored, until she found a seat near the back of the sanctuary. He excused himself and walked towards her, not quite sure what he was doing.

"Good morning, Candace. Is the seat next to you taken?"

Candace jumped, then looked up at him. She shook her head and moved over in the pew so he could sit.

"Welcome to our church. I notice you just kind of sneaked in." His grin met her frown.

"I'm not sure I should even be here, Jonah."

"And why's that?"

She shrugged. "I don't know. I haven't gone to church in years, but your pastor stopped at my table yesterday and invited me."

"As I should have done. I apologize for not doing that."

She searched his face, a frown drawing her brows done. "Why apologize? It's not your place to invite me here."

"But you see, it is." He went to continue the conversation but stopped as the worship team started their music. "We can talk more after church if you like."

Candace nodded even as she shivered. She gave a quick glance around, wondering who it was that had targeted her.

Jonah noted her discomfort and sighed. Okay, Lord, now what? It looks as if You want me to talk to her, but just talk okay? I don't want the adventures that my friends have had. I don't think I could do that.

Candace sat after the service, her mind trying to comprehend what the pastor has spoken on. God's love - she knew she was loved, but he had presented it in a way she had never heard before. She looked up as Jonah stood.

"Listen, some friends and I are going out for a meal. Would you care to join us?"

She studied him for a moment. "Friends?"

He nodded. "There's a group of about eight of us guys that get together when we can. You wouldn't be the only lady there. Five of them are married now. And I think the police chief and his wife are planning on joining us today."

"Why?"

"Why what?" Jonah was honestly surprised at her question.

"Why ask me to join you? You don't know anything about me."

"That's not true." He grinned. "You have my Aunt Lois' approval, and that's hard to get."

She shook her head, hesitation in her manner.

"No pressure. It's okay if you don't want to."

"It's not that. It's just I have a mess to clean up at home and it may take a while."

"Then let me help you. We still need to talk about my supplying you with produce." Jonah grinned again at the look on her face, his hands going up. "Like I said, no pressure."

She shook her head. "I don't think so, not today, but thank you." She turned and walked away from him.

Jonah's eyes followed her as he felt someone stop beside him.

Andrew McBeth, Elmton Police Chief, stopped beside his friend. "What's the story with her, Jonah?"

He shrugged. "What do you mean?"

"I mean, she's new to town, she's assaulted yesterday at the farmer's market, something that never happens, and then when she gets home, her office is tossed."

Jonah spun to stare at his friend. "Her home? Wow! That's what she meant then."

"What's that?"

"She wouldn't come out for a meal with our group, said she had stuff to do at home."

Andrew shook his head. "The patrol officers who responded said she was a tough read. She didn't seem to think anything was missing from her home but she still had to go through it." He paused, looking around for Phoebe, his wife. "Maybe we need to pay her a visit and help."

"And how would we know her address?"

"We know it because she moved in next door to us." Andrew grinned at Jonah's expression. "Come on, pal. Let's find Phoebe and then tell the others we won't be joining them today for a meal."

❦ ❦ ❦ ❦

Candace changed into shorts and a favourite faded T-shirt, then made her way to the kitchen. She shook her head. No, nothing to eat, she thought. Her stomach burned at the thought of someone in her home, going through her files and who knows what else. She headed for the office, then stopped in the doorway, arms crossed, and stared at the mess. She had left it there last night, too tired and heartsick to even look at it. Broken sleep was catching up with her as she yawned, then stepped in the office, staring around, trying to decide where to begin.

The doorbell interrupted her thoughts, and she cast a glance towards the front door, hoping if she ignored them, whoever was there would go away. When it rang the second time, she sighed, then rose from where she had just sat down, making her way towards.

Candace stared at the young couple standing there, then at Jonah.

"Hi. I'm Phoebe. This is my husband, Andrew. We're your next-door neighbours." Phoebe smiled at her. "Jonah said you wouldn't come eat with our group. So, we decided to bring lunch to you." Her head tilted as she watched the emotions flickering across Candace's face.

"I'm sorry. Please come in. I'm Candace. Jonah, did you put them up to this?"

Jonah shook his head. "Nope. Not me. Andrew came up with the plan. But I think it's a great idea. First, we eat. Then, we're here to help you."

She stared at him for a moment, then shook her head. "I guess I'll have to say thank you. The kitchen's this way." She paused as Andrew and Phoebe placed the containers of sandwiches and fruit on the kitchen table. "I'm sorry. I only have water and coffee to offer you."

Andrew held up his hand to stem the words she was trying to get out. "Either one is fine, Candace. We're not fussy."

More relaxed than she had been in months, Candace stood an hour later in her office, looking at the piles of paper and folders.

Andrew whistled. "Matt said they made a mess. He's right." He turned to Candace. "So, how do you want to do this?"

She shrugged. "I have no idea other than the papers will need sorting out again." She sighed. "This is a lot of work for nothing."

"Are you sure it's nothing?" Andrew's quiet question caught her off guard.

She turned, her eyes searching his face. "I'm sure it's nothing. I don't have anything that belongs to anyone else. I know very few people here so far. This is just my work, nothing personal kept in this cabinet." She waved her hand at the pile. "So, I guess, we just dive in. We can use the dining room table to sort." She reached for the top pile of papers when a hand stopped her.

"Let Andrew and I pick this up. We'll bring it into you and Phoebe in the dining room." Jonah's voice was quiet as he spoke.

She looked at him for a moment, then nodded. Andrew and Phoebe shared a look, then a shrug.

Four hours later, flushed with laughter, Candace shoved the last filing drawer closed. What would have taken her all that day to sort had been done in short order, with lots of laugher intermingled with conversation.

Phoebe stood near her and reached out to hug her.

"Thanks for spending time with us today, Candace. I know it's not easy being the new girl on the block."

Candace stepped back. "What do you mean? Weren't you raised here? You seem to know the town so well?"

Phoebe laughed as she shot a look at Andrew, standing in the hall talking with Jonah. "No, I'm not from here. I didn't come here until just before Andrew and I married. Some day, I'll tell you my story."

"A story? Oh my! After what you've said about your friends and their wives, can yours be a story too?"

Phoebe laughed even harder as she felt Andrew's arm slip around her. "Trust me. Ours was an adventure and a half. Let's plan on getting together sometime this week and we'll talk. I'd like to hear more about your company."

"That you can do, but we really need to leave Candace on her own now, Phoebe. I'm sure she wants a break from us. Call us if you need anything at all, Candace. I mean that. We're working on what happened to you. And our force is good. They like to solve mysteries."

Jonah stood for a moment, studying the young woman in front of him, before he spoke. "We still need to discuss my supplying you with produce. Will one day this week work for you to stop by my farm?"

She nodded, her eyes on the tree in her front yard. "That would work. Tuesday is likely best." She moved past him, towards the tree, trying to think of what was different about it.

"Candace?" Jonah kept pace with her. "What's the problem?"

Candace reached for the object on the tree, but Jonah's hand stopped her. He turned, looking for Andrew and motioning him back.

"Don't touch it, Candace. That's not your camera?"

She shook her head as Andrew walked up beside them. Jonah pointed to the camera, and Andrew sighed. Lord, not another one. We just got through this with Samuel and Aideen.

"A camera? I would hazard a guess your visitors left it." Andrew reached for his phone. "I'll have the crime scene tech come and get it. Jonah, stay with her in the house. I'm looking around outside."

Two hours later, Candace finally sank back onto her couch. This is not how she expected her move to Elmton to go. Lord, what are you trying to tell me, she asked? She sighed, her head raising on the back of the couch, her eyes sliding closed as she slept.

The man watching from the neighbour's backyard smiled to himself. He had watched the activity over the last couple of hours and knew she was scared. When the time was right, he would strike.

Chapter 3

$\mathcal{J}$onah turned as he hear a vehicle driving up his laneway on Tuesday and glanced at his watch as he walked away from the drive shed. If that was Candace, she was just on time. He watched as she parked, then slid out of her vehicle. She waved, her fingers locking her door.

"Candace, hi! Glad you were able to make it today?"

"Thanks for asking me to drop by, Jonah." She smiled, even as her eyes searched the property. "Wow! You really do have a lot of produce, don't you?"

"This farm has been going for a number of years. My grandfather used to farm it but Dad turned it into what it is today. We've done well. In the wintertime, we use the greenhouses to provide produce to our customers."

She turned to where he was pointing. "Oh, that's wonderful. A year-round supply! Okay, so, where do we start?"

He laughed as he pointed behind him. "Let's start with this field, and then we'll end up in the greenhouses."

Jonah listened to her quiet, intelligent questions. He could tell she put a lot of thought into what she planned for meals.

Candace finally stood in the middle of one of the greenhouses, watching Jonah as he checked the lettuce, pulling some to hand her.

"I can't take this for free, Jonah!"

"Yes, you can. My friends always know they can have what they want when they want." He grinned at her.

"So, I'm a friend now, am I?"

"Yes, I think you are. So, friend, can I interest you in a coffee before you head out?"

She checked her watch, then shook her head. "I really need to head back. I have a visit planned in about 90 minutes and need to pick up the material I have to take with me." She walked towards the door, stopping when Jonah spoke her name.

"What was that, Jonah?"

"Be very careful. Andrew hasn't said he's found whoever it was that did what they did to you on Saturday. It's not the welcome to town you should have had. You have my number. Call me if you need to."

She started to shake her head, then stopped, her head tilting as she studied the man in front of her, a perplexed look on her face before she finally agreed. Jonah walked with her to her car, shutting the door after her and watching her drive away.

Why do I feel like I just failed her, Lord? What am I to do to make her feel safe here in town? He shook his head as he turned back to his work.

Candace watched Jonah in her rearview mirror, then sighed. She just didn't know what to do anymore, she thought, the gathered her mind back to the upcoming visit.

❦ ❦ ❦ ❦

Jonah grabbed at his phone as it chimed, knocking it to the floor from the kitchen counter. Muttering to himself, he picked it up and frowned. He didn't know that number.

"Hello?" Jonah could hear noise in the background but no voice. "Hello? Is someone there?"

"Be warned. Stay away from her."

"What? Stay away from who?" Jonah frowned as the call ended, staring at his phone for a moment before shrugging and tucking it into his pocket. He had no idea who he had just been warned about.

He heard his collie start barking and headed for the door. As he hit the porch, he heard a yelp from the dog and ran for the back yard. He couldn't see Rusty at first, then found him, cowering near a tree. Jonah bent, hear a growl from Rusty, then was on the ground, face first, as his vision darkened.

How long he had been on the ground, he couldn't tell, but he was chilled, except where Rusty had curled up tight to him. He groaned as he shoved himself to his knees, his hand going to his head. Who had done this and why?

Hand to the back of his head, he curled forward until his other hand was resting on the ground, supporting him. His head pounded with pain. Rusty snuggled up under his arm, his tongue licking Jonah's face as fast as he could.

Jonah finally straightened up and pulled himself to his feet. He stared around, eyes still somewhat blurry, and turned, catching himself before he went down. Heading for his house, he reached for his phone, scowling as he tried to read the digits to call for help.

The patrol officer stood and watched as Ezra, the paramedic, tended to Jonah's head.

"You really need to go to Emerge, Jonah." Ezra was frustrated.

Jonah shook his head and the room spun. The two men with him caught him as he fell sideways.

Ezra pointed at the stretcher. Soon, Jonah was on his way, leaving the patrol officers to search for his assailant.

Ezra monitored his vitals, then hearing a rustle in Jonah's pocket, reached and pulled out a paper. His eyes shot to Jonah's face and closed eyes. What had Jonah walked into, he wondered?

Ezra turned from Jonah's stretcher as he heard footsteps. Andrew walked towards him.

"Ezra, what do we have?"

Ezra shrugged. "Not quite sure, Andrew. Apparently, Jonah was knocked out tonight. We were talking to him in his kitchen, he moved, and passed out. He wasn't able to give much information." He held up the paper he had removed from Jonah's pocket. "I found this on the way in."

Andrew reached for the paper, his eyes first on Ezra, then Jonah. Opening it, he frowned.

"Did you read this?"

Ezra nodded. "Just what has Jonah gotten himself mixed up in?"

Andrew read the note again, which warned Jonah about getting involved in something that was not his business. "Whoever wrote this wasn't real exact, were they?'

Ezra's partner came looking for him at that point. "I don't know much more than what I've told you, Andrew. The patrol officer was still out at Jonah's."

Andrew nodded, his focus on Jonah. "Thanks, Ezra. We'll likely need a statement from you about this note. Stop by the department tomorrow."

Jonah groaned, his hand finding the sore spot on his head again as his eyes opened and he searched.

"Jonah?"

Jonah's head turned and he regretted it. "Andrew? What are you doing here?"

"I was still at the office when the call came in. Tell me what happened."

Jonah sighed. "I can't tell you much other than I went to find Rusty, heard a sound from him, walked towards him and then woke up on the ground. What happened? The last thing I remember was talking to Ezra."

"You passed out again and he brought you in here." Andrew paused. "He also found a note in your pocket."

"A note? That's strange."

"It is. It warns you to stay out of what's not your business."

"That would go with the phone call I got just before I headed outside."

"Phone call?"

"Yeah. I didn't know the number but it warned me about helping her."

"Her? As in who?"

Jonah shrugged as the curtain to the cubicle opened and the physician walked in. "I have no idea, unless maybe Candace?"

Andrew nodded. "It might be. I'll have someone talk to her in the morning. And I'll also have someone stop by to give you a lift home. I understand they're keeping you overnight."

Jonah sighed, knowing he had no choice but not liking it. His head back on the pillow, his eyes closing, he prayed, not for himself, but for the young woman who had walked into his life just a few days before.

❦ ❦ ❦ ❦

Candace looked out from the kitchen in her business and frowned. What was

Andrew doing here and with a patrol officer at that?

"Candace, can we talk?" Andrew stopped before he entered her work space.

Grabbing a towel to dry her hands, Candace walked towards him, a puzzled look on her face. "Sure. What about?"

"Did you get any strange phone calls yesterday?"

She shook her head, her eyes watchful. "No, I haven't." Pulling her phone out, she scrolled through the call list. "Nothing but work. Why?"

Andrew stared past her for a moment. "Jonah got a call last night warning him to stay away from a woman. Then, he was knocked out and a note left in his pocket saying basically the same."

"Is he all right?" Concern laced her voice. "I was out at his place yesterday morning, just on business. We're working up a deal for him to provide fresh vegetables for my clients."

"That's what he said. He didn't see his assailant."

She shook her head. "I have no idea, Andrew, who it would have been."

Andrew sighed, knowing he was at a loss. "Let me know if anything strange happens. If you're uncomfortable at all, call us." He nodded to the officer as he turned, his eyes searching her building.

Candace stood, hands on her hips, before moving back to the kitchen. She paused, staring down at the countertop, not quite sure what was going on. Lord, I have no idea what this is about. I don't have any enemies that I know of. I don't even have any friends here, yet, that would be at risk. So, who is it?

Chapter 4

$\mathcal{J}$onah turned cautiously as he heard a vehicle approaching. He had been out in his fields, trying to work, and not succeeding very well with the pounding headache he had developed. He had refused to take anything, knowing he would only sleep if he did. He watched as two good friends exited the truck.

"Jonah? You okay? You shouldn't be out here." Josiah Silverthorn called as he and Noah Lockwood walked towards him.

"Josiah. Noah. I'm doing okay. What brings you out?"

"Andrew called, asking us to come out and help." Josiah looked around. "What do you need done?"

"Right now, not much. I had pretty much picked everything yesterday. I was planning on heading into town today with the orders."

"Then, that's why we're here. You stand and tell us what to do, then we'll make your deliveries for you." Noah was adamant that Jonah would rest.

"Thanks, guys."

His head back on the truck seat, Jonah's eyes slid closed as he waited for Noah to come back out from the last delivery. He was exhausted and he knew he wouldn't sleep tonight. The headache hadn't eased at all. If anything, it had gotten worse. He knew he would be needing to take pain medications and he didn't want to.

Noah stood for a moment, studying his friend, trying to decide whether he should have him come back to his place, or if he should volunteer to stay with him tonight. He sighed. Jonah was stubborn and would probably say he didn't need anyone, but Noah knew better.

"Jonah?"

Noah's voice filtered through the pain. He raised his head, his eyes narrowed against the sun. "Yeah, Noah?"

"Look, you shouldn't be by yourself."

Jonah shook his head, wincing as he did so. "Just take me home, please, Noah. I can take something and sleep now."

Noah stared at him, then through the window, finally pulling away from the cafe. He searched his mind as to who he could call for help and then shook his head again. No matter who he called, Jonah would not be pleased with him

❦ ❦ ❦ ❦

Four hours later, Noah stood and walked to the front door in answer to a knock. He watched the red-haired beauty who stood there for a moment, before she turned back.

"Can I help you?" Noah had a good idea of who this was.

"I'm Candace, and you, I think, are Noah. Jonah described his friends to me. How is Jonah?" Candace's eyes searched Noah's face.

Noah stepped back, motioning her into the house. "I think he's finally sleeping. I talked him into some pain meds."

"It's that bad, the headache?"

34

Noah nodded. "It is. He's to the point he can't move without it hurting."

Candace nodded, then looked down at the basket she held. "I brought some food for him, but I don't think he'll be eating yet, will he?"

Noah shook his head as he pointed to the kitchen. "Let's put it in the fridge for him. He's stretched out in the living room."

Candace stopped, before she headed for that room. She stood for a moment, her eyes searching Jonah's face, seeing the pain lines etched there.

"Noah, does he have an ice pack?"

"I'm sure he does. Why?"

"Can you get it for me along with a towel?" She reached to take it from Noah when he returned, wrapping the pack in the small towel and then gently tucking it under Jonah's neck. She hesitated as she heard him groan, then a few seconds later heard the sigh of relief as the cold started to ease the pain.

"A cold pack on the neck?"

Candace nodded. "With concussions, you can get migraine-like headaches. My mom suffers from migraines and a cold pack always makes her feel better." She turned to him. "Now, what can I do to help?"

Noah shrugged. "I'm not really sure, Candace. I'm planning on staying overnight, just to watch him."

"Good, because so am I." She headed for the kitchen, setting her basket on the table and stuffing the food containers into the fridge. "Now, what can you tell me about what happened?"

Noah just shrugged once more. "Not a lot. He didn't see who hit him. Whoever it was took a good kick at Rusty."

"Rusty. Where is he?"

"On the back deck. Hey, wait, Jonah doesn't let him in."

"Too bad, because that's where he needs to be, with Jonah."

Noah watched as Rusty hesitated at the door, then raced through to find Jonah, his tongue licking at Jonah's face until a quiet word from Candace sent him to the floor, muzzle on his paws, eyes on his master.

"How'd you do that? Even Jonah can't get him to behave like that?"

"What, making him mind? He's like a two-year-old child. You just need the right tone of voice." Candace shot him a quick look, before her eyes went back to study Jonah. She reached for the ice pack, repositioning it.

"Candace?" When she looked at him, Noah spoke. "Do you know what happened to him or why?"

She sighed before she shook her head. She walked back to the kitchen to the back door, her face thoughtful.

"Not really, other than he came to my aid a couple of days ago. Why someone would target him because of that, I have no idea." She turned, her eyes searching Noah's face.

"What was that about then?"

She shrugged. "I have no idea. I'm new to town, just here for about three months. Before that I had a very boring life, no boyfriend, just work."

"If that's the case, why come after you? Jonah seemed to think it was pretty personal."

Her eyes round, Candace stared at him. "He talked about it?"

Noah nodded. "He did. He wanted to get a sense from us what it might have been about.   He has a tender heart, Candace. Don't hurt him."

She shook her head. "I would never do that intentionally, Noah."   She paused, biting at her right index fingernail.   "I wonder."

"You wonder what?"   Noah's head tilted as he studied her.

"I wonder if it could be. Years ago, I received a letter from a lawyer, telling me that I was the long lost niece of someone who had invented something or other. I just ignored it. I know my family, my aunts and uncles and none of them fit that category."

"That's strange. But if that's the case, why would it start up again?"

She shrugged, pulling out her phone, then pausing as she heard a groan from Jonah. They both moved that way, finding

Jonah sitting up, Rusty's chin on his leg, his hand on Rusty's head.

"Jonah?" Noah's question brought his head up. "How's the head?"

"Still there, if you really want to know. But the ice pack helped. Thanks."

"That was Candace's doing, Jonah."

"Thank her for me when you see her, okay?"

Noah's eyes met Candace's. Her eyes sparkled with mirth.

"You're welcome, Jonah."

He groaned as he raised his head. "You're here?"

"I am. Now, let Noah help you get cleaned up. I have some food I think will sit just right in your stomach."

Jonah stood, staggered, then allowed Noah to help him walk. "What happened?"

"What happened is that you took some pain meds and faded out on us." Noah pointed him to the washroom. "Go, clean up. Candace brought some food for you."

"She did?" Jonah turned towards the kitchen, stopping when Noah's hand came up to his shoulder. "Right. Clean up. Then eat. How powerful was that medication, anyway?"

Noah just laughed, then turning, caught the look on Candace's face. "It's okay. He just can't handle strong medication. He's apt to say or do anything."

She frowned, then shook her head. "I don't know about that. He seems rather unsteady on his feet."

"He will be until it wears off. But his eyes are clearer than they were." Noah retrieved the ice pack and returned it to the freezer. "Now, what can I do to help with the food?"

Jonah finally sat his spoon down on the table, feeling much more like himself. "I don't know what was in that soup, Candace, but it was delicious and certainly helped clear my head."

She smiled and shook her head. "Not telling. It's an old family recipe that I've adapted." She looked at the two men. "Now, what do we do about what happened?"

"Do? We leave it to Andrew and his officers, of course." Noah watched her reaction, his eyes narrowing as she shook her head.

"No, we can't. They're overworked as it is. Now, I wonder." She pulled out her phone once again. "Jace? How are you? Naomi? Oh, that's wonderful. Now, is Em around? She's at home? No, I have the number. I'll call her there. What's that? No, I'm behaving. You're the one who's always up to no good. Thanks." She was laughing as she ended the call. Jace was a good friend as was his wife, Naomi. She needed to head there way soon.

She paused, then dialled another number, the two men watching in silence before sharing a look. "Emma? Hi! How are you? I'm good. Yes, you do need to come over. Now, I have something I need you to run for me. Do you remember that letter I got? Yes, that one. You did. And? Okay, I just thought…." Her voice trailed off as a troubled look came over her face. "If you could. When are you and Abe heading this way? Saturday? Oh, that's great. I look forward to that. No, I should be home. Thanks again." She closed the case on her phone after ending the call and slipped it back into her pocket.

"Candace?" Jonah's quiet voice raised her head, the question he wanted to ask but wouldn't hanging in the air.

"That's my cousin, Emma. She has a business where she searches for things. She's been quietly looking into that letter now for years and has news." She searched Jonah's face and then Noah's.

"Just who is Emma, Candace?"

Noah's question made her sigh. "Not many people, other than her friends, know this about her. She keeps that part of her life separate from her personal life." She bit her lip, trying to decide what to say as the men studied her. "If you've heard of Trackers, then you've heard of Emma. Please, don't tell anyone. She wants that part of her life private."

The men shared a glance. They had both heard of Tracker, but didn't realize she was related to Candace. Noah, studying her, saw the resemblance.

"What has she found out?" Jonah's voice brought Candace's head up.

"I don't know. She and her husband, Abe, are heading this way from Riverville on Saturday."

Jonah nodded. "I want to meet with you and them. This involves me now."

She nodded, her eyes on Noah's face. She tilted her head, wondering at the look she saw there.

"Noah?"

He shook his head as his attention came back to the room. "I think I met your cousin years ago. At least, I think it was her. She was with a man named Jace. We had all been working on a hacking in a high-profile company."

"That would have been her. Jace's mother rescued her from the streets and took her in. She doesn't share her life story with many."

"No, she doesn't. Listen, Jonah? Are you going to be all right now if I leave?" Noah stood and began to gather their dishes.

"I will. Thanks again, Noah, for all you and Josiah did today."

Noah shrugged off his thanks. "That's what friends do. I know Samuel and

Matthias are planning on stopping by tomorrow. Put them to work, okay."

Jonah nodded as he watched Noah walk away, then turned to Candace. "Thank you, too, Candace. What you've done for a virtual stranger.." He stopped speaking as she shook her head.

"It's okay, Jonah. Somehow, I think what happened to you is related to me. I have to run as well."

"Call me when you get home? I want to know you made it safely."

She stared at him for a moment before nodding.

Jonah watched her walk away, his heart bowed in prayer for her. He had no idea where this was going, but he knew that she needed to feel the love of God in a tangible way that night.

Chapter 5

*S*aturday morning found Candace pacing her living room, arms wrapped tight around herself. She had found two more letters in the mail at her office and handed them over to Andrew. She was scared, she admitted it to herself. She was also afraid that whoever it was would escalate to the point her new friends would be hurt even more. And that she couldn't handle.

She turned as she heard the doorbell, hesitating, her mind whirling. She snuck a peek out the door and breathed a sigh of relief. It was Jonah, early of course.

Jonah grinned as he saw Candace open the door, but the grin faded as he saw the dark circles under her eyes.

"Candace? Are you okay?" He closed the door behind him as she stepped backwards.

She shook her head. "Not really. I had two more letters come to my office."

"Two! Were you threatened?"

She shook her head. "No. They just asked for the information I have. And I have no idea what that is, before you ask." She stopped, her hand going to her mouth. "I'm sorry, Jonah. I shouldn't have snapped at you."

"Hey, it's okay. We're in this together, aren't we?"

She stared at him. "I guess we are and not by your making. Maybe we should just keep our distance from one another."

"Not happening, Candace. That's not who I am or how I treat my friends." He walked past her. "Is it okay if I make some coffee?"

She shook her head as she followed him. "It's all set. Just turn on the pot." She headed for the cupboard and pulled out cups. "You and Abe will be drinking the coffee. Emma and I will be having tea. That's what I prefer sometimes, by the way, English or Irish tea if possible."

Jonah snuck a peek at her, then nodded. "That's good to know. I'll make sure to stock up on it."

She spun, eyes wide at his comment. "Stock up on it?"

He nodded. "That's what I said." He stopped, his eyes searching hers. "Regardless of what happens, I consider you my friend and that's what I do for my friends. And just maybe, one day, you'll agree to go out with me." He winked as he said that.

"Jonah! We don't know each other that well."

"I know what I need to, Candace, and I like what I see. By the way, Josiah mentioned that Faith has asked about you. They would like to meet you."

She shook her head. "What have I done? I don't do this."

Jonah stopped her with a hand on her arm. "There's no rush, Candace. They understand that you're going through stuff." He started to laugh. "In fact, five of my friends and their ladies went through an adventure, shall we call it, as did Andrew and Phoebe."

She groaned. "Tell me it wasn't like Abe and Emma."

"Why? Did they have an adventure too?"

She nodded. "Let me fill you in before they get here. It will have to be quick though." She threw a quick look at the clock. "They're both very punctual and are likely almost here. They married when they were almost finished college, got separated by Emma's step uncle, met up again ten years ago and the rest is history as they said. Emma though Abe was dead, Abe that Emma didn't want anything to do with him."

Jonah shook his head. "That bad? Wow! How did they make it through all those years?"

"God. He kept them strong, moved Emma to Riverville and then they met one day in the police chief's office." She turned as she heard the doorbell and then the door open. "And that will be them. I just wanted you to know."

"Thank you for sharing."

Candace turned as she heard her name called and was hugging her cousin in short order. Abe stood and watched, then held out a hand to Jonah.

"Morning. I'm Abe Findlay. Cousin by marriage to Candace."

"I'm Jonah Bronson. Somehow or other, I got mixed up in this and have no idea what this is."

Abe grinned. "Welcome to the club. I've seen this before, many times." He turned to hug Candace. "Candace. You're supposed to come visit us. Do we need to take you back to our home and provide security for you?"

She groaned. "Please, not that. I wouldn't have a life, not with your guys around."

Abe and Emma started laughing, Jonah staring at the three of them.

Abe took pity on him. "I run a security team of seven plus myself. The seven men consider Candace a younger sister to them all and would be very happy to protect her."

"Smother me, you mean." She pointed at the kitchen. "Abe, Jonah's made coffee for you two. Em, I have your favourite tea. Oh you didn't, did you?"

Emma nodded as she retrieved the box from the table in the entry. "I did. Rylee heard we were coming this way and sent a selection of treats for you."

Candace reached for the box that read The Irish Charm and shook her head. "Nope, not sharing."

Jonah stared at her as the three began to laugh.

"That's a bakery, Jonah. Rylee is married to a good friend of ours. Just wait until you taste her baking. You'll be driving the two hours to get more."

Finally, Emma sat back, her eyes on Abe, who nodded. Emma sighed, not wanting to ruin the good time they'd been having, but she knew she had to talk to her cousin. She studied her for the moment, seeing red hair a richer red than her own russet curls, golden highlights flickering in the sunlight, the eyes the same gray as hers.

"Candace?" Emma's voice was quiet, but Candace still sat up straighter.

"What did you find out, Emma?"

Abe reached for the folder he had set on the floor under his chair and handed it to Emma.

"This. Whoever is doing this is good but not as good as us. Jace has cracked the facade he's been hiding behind."

"Okay. It's he?"

Emma nodded. "It is. Not a relative, which I think you already figured out." Candace nodded at that. "So, what we have is a company he's set up, a dummy corporation, under layers of dummy corporations. This is what we've found so far." She handed Candace the folder. "I know we lost touch years ago and I regret that. We were such good friends when we were kids."

"We lost touch when your aunt married that monster, hubby number 3, wasn't it?"

Emma nodded. "That we did, but that's neither here nor there. What we have here is someone from outside the family who thinks he should have a part of a company that never existed."

"Wait a minute!" Jonah broke into the conversation. "There was never a company?"

Candace shook her head. "Dad was a farmer, not into high-tech stuff, which this guy thinks he was. This person is adamant that Dad created some company and stole ideas from him. The police looked into it years ago and talked to that man. But why all of sudden is he back?"

Abe nodded. "That's what we'd like to know. Jace is working on tracking where he's been and it looks as if he was hospitalized for a number of years."

Candace drew in a breath. "So, he's not stable then?"

"We have no way of knowing where he was or why. We can't access those kinds of records. But we will talk to your police chief here and leave this information with him."

"Thank you. Now, would you two like a tour of my kitchen?"

Abe grinned, winking at his wife. "But we're sitting in your kitchen already."

Candace shook her head at him as she stood. "Not this one. Come on. I know you'll be wanting to head back soon."

Jonah stood for a moment, not sure what to do, before Candace turned to him and reached for his hand. "You too, Jonah. You need to see where I'll be putting your produce to good use."

Jonah closed the door after Candace and stood for a moment, his eyes on her. Abe and Emma shared a look and a smile. They could see the interest there, even if Candace hadn't yet.

Emma walked through her cousin's business, questions coming non-stop. Abe took time to study her security system and nodded.   Good, he thought, she has an excellent one. Joseph, his security expert, would be glad to hear that. It was one question he had asked Abe to answer for him.

Jonah stopped beside Abe, watching as he stood looking around the reception area of the business.

"What are your thoughts?"

Jonah's quiet question stopped Abe for a moment. "I don't like this, Jonah. Emma's worried about her cousin. They were almost like sisters growing up."

Jonah nodded. "I understand. How do we keep her safe? She's here most mornings on her own and then making deliveries or sourcing products or handling interviews with new clients. She's out there alone."

Abe nodded. "I know. There's not much we can do about that. We can't put someone with her 24/7. Your police chief, how much is he aware of this?"

"He knows everything, I would hazard a guess, and has someone working it. The thing is, we don't know how I got involved in this, other than coming to her aid that one day."

Abe nodded. "That's all it would take." He turned as the door chimed and someone entered.

"Andrew! We were just talking about you." Jonah's greeting had Abe relaxing. "Have you met Abe Findlay?"

"Never had the pleasure. What brings you to town?"

Abe pointed over his shoulder. "Candace. Emma and she are cousins, and Emma had some information for her. We have a copy for you as well."

"Emma? Why would she be investigating this?"

Abe sighed. "If I tell you, you have to promise to keep it quiet. Emma doesn't mix her personal life and business one." He watched as Andrew frowned, his eyes on the two women. Then his frown cleared as he recognized Emma.

"Now I understand." Andrew studied Candace for a moment. "Has she said anything about the two new letters?"

Jonah shook his head. "Other than that you had them, no."

Andrew sighed. "Whoever it is has escalated his demands. He wants to meet with her."

"Not happening." Abe and Jonah spoke at the same time.

Andrew laughed, drawing the attention of the two women.

"Emma, love, come and meet Andrew." Abe held out his hand. "I was just telling him you had some information for him."

"Hello, Andrew. Yes, we do have information for you. I had it here somewhere. Where did I put it, Abe?"

"Over there on the desk, love."

She nodded. "Sorry, being here with Candace and seeing what's she accomplished has scrambled my brain for a moment."

Abe gave her a look and then shared one with Candace. There was no way that was what had happened. He would be talking with his wife later.

"Listen, we need to run. Candace, don't be a stranger. The guys and their ladies all want you to come for a visit."

Candace snorted, causing Abe and Emma to start laughing, and the other men to stare at her. "Like that's going to happen? No. They just want to interrogate me, that's all. Tell them I'll be around at some point, some time, in the future."

Abe and Emma gave her a hug, the two men a wave, and walked out. Andrew watched them, then turned back to Candace.

"Give me a recap of what your cousin found."

Candace handed him the folder. "Here. Emma always has a recap of what she's found on the top. Read that. Then you can talk to us about what you've found."

Andrew searched her face, then nodded, walking away from the couple as he read. Jonah watched her face, then catching her hand, walked her to the kitchen.

"Talk to me, Candace."

She shook her head. "It's too dangerous for you to stay friends with me, Jonah."

"I'm not walking away, Candace. I've already told you that. What information has Emma given you?"

Candace shook her head as she moved around her work area, opening cabinets and drawers and then closing them. She walked to the large refrigerator and did the same, stopping with the freezer door open, studying what was inside. She finally sighed, a decision made, turning to him just as Andrew walked towards him.

"I would really like to know how they found this information, Candace. They've found stuff we haven't been able to."

"It's all done legally, Andrew. They have the resources and security clearances well above what you have. Emma's is even higher than Abe's and his is really high."

He nodded. "I wasn't questioning that, Candace. It's just we've been looking and haven't found what she has." His eyes traced into the distance, not seeing the window he was looking at. "Did she tell you anything?"

She nodded. "Yes, she did and no, I don't know that man or his family. I'm sure I've never ever met them. My Dad isn't into technology, except where it can help his farm. And that is limited. He doesn't have shares in any company that we know of."

Andrew nodded, his eyes now on Jonah, who was watching Candace intently. He sighed. Here we go again, Lord, and I know just how he feels. Protect them both.

"So, why come after you?"

She shrugged. "I have no idea. This has been ongoing since I turned 18. And no, I don't own any shares in anything either. Not our thing." She stared at Andrew, her brow furrowed in concentration. "So, why? Emma couldn't get a good read on why, either, and that's so unlike her. She's still digging as is Jace." She paused as her phone chimed. "It's Jace. Hi, Jace. What's up? You do. Okay, let me put you on speaker. The chief of police is here with Jonah and I." She paused as she listened for a moment, her eyes on Jonah.

"Okay, I can do that. Thanks."

Andrew and Jonah waited for her to speak but when she didn't, Andrew sighed.

"Is there anything you need to tell me?"

She shook her head. "Not right at the moment. Jace is still working through some stuff. He just wanted some more information from me that I don't have here."

Andrew nodded, his face thoughtful. "You need to keep me in the loop, Candace. No going off on your own, you hear?" He kept his eyes locked on her until she nodded.

"Good, then we understand one another. We'll see each other tomorrow then."

Candace leaned against the counter as she watched him walk away, then sighed, her gaze going to Jonah, who stood, hands in his jeans' pocket, eyes on her.

"What? Aren't you even going to ask?"

He shook his head. "I trust you, Candace, to tell me what I need to know."

She studied him, then nodded. "Okay, so now what?"

"I need to get back to the farm. Faith and Josiah ran my booth this morning, but I have work to do. Care to join me?"

"I would love to, but I have work to do at home." She sighed once more. "More work than I really want to do or care to do, but it's calling my name and I must oblige it."

Chapter 6

*A*rms crossed against her abdomen, Candace stood in her reception area, watching the crime scene techs work in her business. She had walked into a mess that morning, security system disabled, office torn apart. She hadn't been into the kitchen yet to see what it was like, but she had a good idea it wouldn't be in the pristine shape she had left it two days ago.

Andrew walked towards her, listening to what Bill, one of his detectives, was saying. He stopped just short of the door, his eyes searching the mess.

"Candace?"

She spun at his voice. "Andrew. Didn't expect to see you here."

"I had an early morning meeting but came as soon as I could. Do you know if anything missing?"

She shook her head. "I can't tell yet, Andrew. Why me?"

Bill and Andrew shared a look. "It may be related to what happened to you over a week ago and the letters you've received. Someone is looking for something."

"And if I knew what it was, I'd let them have it." She turned as she heard Andrew's name called and he excused himself to walk to the kitchen.

A few quiet words with the tech and she saw him spin and stare at her, before coming towards her.

"Candace, where were you yesterday evening?"

"At the Bible study at the church and then I did go for coffee with them. Why?"

Andrew pointed behind him. "Because there's a body in your freezer. The tech thinks sometime during the evening."

"A body? As in dead?" As his nod, she began to shake. "Who?"

"We don't know that yet. I'll have to ask you to go with Bill. He'll need to take you downtown and get a statement from you." He waited until she nodded, then looked up Bill.

Bill waited for Candace to catch up her purse and briefcase, then followed her, closing his car door after her, eyes searching the neighbourhood. He had heard about Candace from Josiah, but hadn't expected to meet her this way. He had a quiet word with Andrew, then slid behind the wheel of his car, his eyes searching Candace's face, taking in the shudders running through her.

"This shouldn't take long. Then I'll have someone run you home."

She finally nodded. "There's an appointment book on the front desk. Can someone grab that for me when there's a chance. I have a computer schedule but I need to compare the two." She sighed. "I'm guessing I won't be making any meals for a few days."

Bill shook his head. "Not likely. We'll have a clean up team go through there but any food stuffs will need to be disposed of."

She nodded again. "There goes any profit I had for this month."

"It's that tight for you?"

She sighed. "I had just started up about three months ago, building clientele. It takes time to make a profit. I was fortunate enough to already done that. There's a need here for what I provide. Now, I have no idea if my clientele will even stay with me, given what they found."

Bill shrugged. "It's a small town, Candace. They'll have heard of you, heard your reputation, heard what you're doing for those who can't for themselves. I don't think you'll have to worry."

"But I will. I have clients expecting meals tonight, and I don't have them ready to deliver. In fact, I don't have anywhere I can make them."

"Let's get your statement. Then I have an idea."

She turned to look him, a frown on her face.

"No, don't ask yet. I have to make some phone calls. I'll do that while Lily's taking your statement."

She watched as Bill walked away after introducing her to Lily. Lily frowned. This was not like Bill to do this. She shrugged, then pointed to her office.

"Let's get your statement and then see where we go."

An hour later, Candace sat back, feeling drained as she signed her name to her statement

"Is that it, then?"

Lily nodded, then watched as Candace rose.

"Thank you, Lily. Now, if you'll excuse me, I need to get home and see what I can come up with for meals for tonight." She turned to walk away, stopping when Lily spoke.

"Bill asked that you wait for him."

Candace spun, her eyes on Lily. "Thank you, but no. I have too much to do." She turned and walked out of the department, heading for her home.

"Lily, where's Candace?" Bill stood beside her.

"You just missed her."

Bill muttered to himself and then ran for his car, his eyes searching for Candace.

Pulling to a stop in front of her, he rolled down the window.

"Get in, Candace." When she just stood watching him, he repeated himself. "Get in. I've found somewhere you can work to make your meals for today. It's a little diner here in town. Ev will let you work there."

She shrugged, then slid into the seat.

"Why?"

"Why what? Why will she let you work there? Because she's the aunt of one of our friends and takes care of us all. That's why."

"That doesn't make a whole lot of sense, you know."

"It's who she is. She's quite a character and well loved. She wants to do this."

"I'll repay her. What? I can't do that either?"

Bill was shaking his head. "She'll want no payment, Candace."

"Just who is she, Bill? If you don't tell me, I'll go nowhere with you."

He sighed. "She's Andrew's Aunt Ev."

"Did he set this up?"

"No, I did, but he would have if he'd had time."

❧ ❧ ❧ ❧

Ev watched as Candace concentrated on her recipe before turning to Bill.

"How long does Andrew think she'll be out of her kitchen?"

Bill shrugged. "At least a couple of days. But then I'm not sure she'll want to go back there. All her produce and supplies will have to be thrown out."

Ev nodded. "Talk to Silas and then the mayor. Use our town fund for helping to resupply her. Here, take this to start the fund." Eve slipped him a cheque.

"Thank you, Ev. She's not going to want to take this."

"Then we'll have to convince her. Who....?" Her voice died away as the door opened and Jonah walked in with crates of produce for her, stopping as he saw Candace.

Jonah frowned, setting the crate down on the counter, before walking towards Candace, waiting to speak until she looked up.

"Move addresses, Candace?" He was genuinely puzzled at her being here.

She blew out a breath. "I had to. I had a break-in and they found a body in my freezer."

"A body?" Jonah stopped speaking, studying here. "When?"

She shrugged. "This morning. The tech thinks sometime last night. And I had to come up with an alibi." Tears sparkled near the surface of her eyes before she looked back down at her recipe, her thoughts going back to what she was preparing.

"Candace?" When she didn't look up, he spoke again. "Candace, did you tell them you were with our Bible study group until late?"

She nodded, not looking up. "It doesn't matter, Jonah. Excuse me, please. I need to get this done so I can do my deliveries."

"But where's your car?"

She sighed. "Behind the crime scene tape, I would suspect. I'll figure out something."

Jonah looked up to see Bill watching him. He walked towards him.

"Bill?"

"Ev volunteered to help as much as she can. She's already having some of her suppliers stop by to begin the process of restocking Candace's kitchen. We're also working on the money for it."

Jonah nodded. "But with her car at the business, she'll have no way to deliver what she's working so hard at, unless she takes a taxi, and that will add up."

Bill held up a hand. "Ev's already taken care of that. Avery's here today and volunteered to chauffeur her. Then the ladies of our group have offered their help as well. I'm expecting Paige and Phoebe here by noon to help."

"Can we do that? What about the regulations these two work under?"

"Ev called Simon and cleared it. He's working on a temporary licensing for them to do just that. The thing is, Paige and

Phoebe have taken this training, without us knowing about it."

"Then, that works. Listen, I have to run. I've got more deliveries to make. Can you keep me in the loop as much as you can?"

Bill nodded before he approached Candace.

"Candace?" When she looked up, he spoke again. "We'll work through who it was. I'll be in touch as soon as I know more. Don't worry. We don't think it was you." He looked around, his eyes stopping on Avery, Andrew's cousin, who worked not far from Candace. "Avery has volunteered to help you make your deliveries today. We'll get your car back to you as soon as we can."

She sighed, leaning against the stainless steel countertop. "I forgot. I was so concerned about the meals that I forgot about how I was going to deliver them. I'm going to owe everyone big time."

"No, you won't. You're part of our church family. This is what we do. It's how we put feet and hands to be servants for God."

She stared at him. "I've never heard it put that way again. My parents raised me that way." She sighed again. "How long will I be out of my business."

He shrugged. "For a few days. Then I'll send in a team to clean out the supplies and clean up well for you."

She nodded. "Thank you." Her voice was quiet.

He watched for a moment before turning and walking away to try and find answers.

Why, Lord? Why did this happen to a lady one of my friends is interested in? And not again. We've had enough adventures, haven't we? But You know best. You have that plan and purpose in place.

❧ ❧ ❧ ❧

Candace heard her name called as she finished packing the meals she had prepared and looked up, surprise on her face.

"Ian! Murphy! What are you two doing here?" She sprang towards them to be enveloped in hugs.

"Emma said you had some problems. Abe sent us." Murphy dropped a kiss on her cheek.

"I have had, but this town has picked up for me. That still doesn't explain you two showing up."

Ian grinned as he hugged her as well. "Emma sent us. She wanted to make sure you were okay."

She nodded, unable to speak for tears. "That Emma! Aren't you two out on a mission or something?"

They both shook their heads, then looked past her as Avery approached. She was quick to introduce them.

"Avery was just about to help me deliver the meals. Can you two stay for a while?"

The two men exchanged looks and nodded. "Just let us have your address and we'll meet you there."

"You two are up to something, aren't you? How much of a security system did you bring with you?"

Ian laughed. "You'll see. Abe asked that we go over your home. We'll come back to see to your business once you have it back."

She pulled out her extra house key. "Here. Let yourselves in. Your ladies didn't come?"

"No, they wanted to but had other commitments. They've all asked us to bring you home at some point."

She nodded. "Yes, I do need to do that. We'll work on that." She turned to Avery. "All set? Then let's get these meals to my people."

Avery watched as the two men walked away, then turned to Candace as he drove away.

"I take it you know these men well?" Avery was in law enforcement and did everything he could to protect those he came in contact with.

"I do. They're part of a security team my cousin's husband runs over in Riverville. I haven't seen them in about six months. I miss them all." Her voice turned reflective and she stared out the window at the passing buildings.

Avery nodded, even though she couldn't see him. He intended to research that team. He remembered the look on Jonah's face that morning and wanted to ensure his friend wouldn't get hurt.

Chapter 7

$\mathcal{J}$onah knocked at Candace's door early that evening. He had finished what he needed to do and headed back into town. Candace was beginning to mean a lot to him and he wanted to make sure she was handling what she had gone through.

He turned as the door open and a man around his age stood there. He blinked, not expecting it.

"You must be Jonah. Candace said you'd likely be in. Come on in. We're just getting ready to eat, if you haven't yet. I'm Ian, by the way, a friend."

Jonah followed him silently to the back deck, where he saw Candace laughing at something Murphy had said. She turned, then came towards him to hug him.

"Thank you, Jonah. I'm not sure what part you played in today, but someone was looking after me."

He stood for a moment, searching her face. "I didn't do much. It was Bill. He reached out for you." He looked up to see the two men watching him. "Care to introduce me?"

She nodded as she turned in his arms. "These are two dear friends, Jonah. You met Ian when he let you in. This is Murphy. They work for Abe."

Jonah relaxed. "Good evening. I take it Abe sent you."

The three laughed, drawing a questioning look from him.

"Actually, it was Emma." Murphy grinned. "She was worried about her. We didn't know what had happened until we got here."

Jonah nodded again as they sat to eat. "Any word yet, Candace?"

She shook her head. "Bill figured it would be a couple of days yet. I can't even get my car from the lot."

"Not a problem, Candace. We'll find transportation for you." Jonah shared a look with the other two men, whose eyes had grown stern.

Candace watched a little bit later as Ian and Murphy drove away, with promises from her that she would come and visit soon. Jonah watched, then reached to pull her into a hug.

"Are you sure you're okay?"

She nodded. "I'm getting there. Why would someone do that?"

Jonah shrugged. "Likely to try and stop your business or to frame you or something."

She leaned back to look up at him. "Which one is it? You're tossing out some ideas there."

He laughed as he released her to turn and pick up their dishes and help clean up. "I did, didn't I? Did Bill say when he'd be in touch?"

"No, he didn't. And I do need my car."

"Not tomorrow. We have friends who are going to be here to pick you up and take you where you need to be. Don't protest. It's what we do."

"Bill said basically the same thing this morning." She paused, her hand on the kitchen tap. "Ev has had her suppliers come in and talk to me, giving me really good deals on supplies. Why, Jonah?"

"Because you're part of our community now, Candace. Now, is that it for cleaning up? If it is, I need to run, but I'll be back in tomorrow."

"I'm sure you will be. Thanks, Jonah."

He nodded, his eyes searching hers. "Lock up after me and make sure you set the security system Murphy installed for you."

She sighed. "That I will. He'll never let me live it down if I don't."

He turned to study her face. "They really care about you, don't they?"

She nodded. "I met them after Abe and Emma found each other again. They're like big brothers to me, and their wives are all so great."

Jonah nodded, wondering again how she had ended up here and not there. Maybe one day she'd tell him

❧ ❧ ❧ ❧

Four days later, Candace stood in her business, arms folded around her, as she

78

studied the space. She really didn't want to be there, but knew she had to. She sighed. Okay, Lord, now what? Where do I go? Do I really want to stay here or do I move, yet again, to a new town and start over? I am getting so tired of that. The sound of the door opening startled her and she spun.

Phoebe McBeth stood there, her eyes on Candace.

"Good morning, Candace. I've come to help you get set back up. Andrew mentioned that you had a ton of supplies arriving today and he thought you could use some help."

"Phoebe, thank you. You don't know what this means."

"I've got a pretty good idea. Now, no gloom or doom. No having second thoughts. No worrying out who's out to get you. Those thoughts aren't allowed today."

Candace laughed, even as she moved towards the kitchen. "And what would you be knowing about those kinds of thoughts?"

"Because I went through what our guys call an adventure. It wasn't fun, Candace, not when I was kidnapped, assaulted and injured. And especially not when I married a total stranger to save my life."

Candace spun, her eyes wide. "No way. There's no way you did that."

Phoebe nodded, her eyes thoughtful. "I did. Andrew literally saved my life one night by getting me out of a situation, and then, on Silas' suggestion and with a lot of prayer, we married the next afternoon. And at the time, I was speechless, too traumatized to talk."

Candace stared at her. "Some day, I want to hear the whole story of that."

"And some day I'll tell you. Now, I know we have Silas, Noah's Uncle Seth, and some of the ladies heading our way. Draw up a plan for us, Candace, so we're not tripping over one another all day."

Candace nodded, even as she looked up and saw a supplier's rep standing there. Thanks to Ev and the money the town had provided to her, she would be in better shape than before. Whoever was after her would be disappointed that she hadn't run once more.

Andrew stood later that afternoon, his arm around Phoebe, as he watched Candace move among the people gathered there, thanking each one.

"How is she?" His question was quiet.

"She's afraid, Andrew, but trying hard not to show it. One of who was it, Abe, that's it, Abe's men showed up today and upgraded her security system. The rest of the day, she tried to hide her fear, but I could see it. Maybe because I know what it's like."

"I'm sure she is scared. Did Jonah come through?"

She shook her head. "No, he didn't, but Candace mentioned that he had to be out of town today for something. They did talk on the phone though. They're good for one another."

Andrew smiled as he nodded. "They are. Now, let's head home, love. We need to start clearing out people so that Candace can lock up."

"You're not leaving her here on her own, are you?"

He shook his head as he moved them towards Candace. "No, Jason Long will be here shortly to make sure she gets home safely."

❧ ❧ ❧ ❧

Candace stood at the front desk in the police department two days later, a stressed look on her face. She had asked for either Bill or Lily and was told they weren't in that day. The desk officer had turned away from her for a moment, and she hesitated, not quite sure what to do. She looked down at the envelope in her hand and finally sighed, waiting for him to turn back to her.

"Can I leave this with you for either one of them, then?" She handed it to him as he nodded. "I really need them to get it as soon as they can. Thank you."

She stood on the steps, not quite sure where to head. Whoever was doing this to her had just upped the ante, as they say, she thought. Why threaten Jonah? They were just friends in a group of friends, weren't they? She headed for her car, not seeing the man standing across the street watching her.

She pulled to a stop behind Jonah's truck and still hesitated, not sure if she should be there. She locked her door as she walked away from her car, her eyes searching for Jonah. She heard a low bark and turned to see Rusty running towards her, his tail wagging.

"Where is he, boy? Can you show me?" Candace stood for a moment, her hand on Rusty's head before she moved forward, Rusty tight to her side. "You gonna show me where he is?"

Jonah stood outside the closest greenhouse watching as Rusty led Candace towards him, a frown on his face. He hadn't expected to see her today, not on a Saturday.

"Candace?" His call raised her head and she waved as she walked towards him. "You're out here."

She laughed. "I am. I needed to talk to you, but I'm interrupting your work."

He shrugged. "Come on in. I need about thirty minutes, and then I'm done for the day. Have a seat." He pointed at the stool he had sitting in the building.

She sat, watching as he moved through the plants, a frown in place. Her worry was how she would tell him what that letter has said and how he would react. She pulled out her phone as it chimed.

"Bill?"

"Candace. Where are you?"

"I'm sitting in one of Jonah's greenhouses. I have to talk to him."

She could hear a sigh of relief from Bill. "Good. You're not alone."

"Bill, you're scaring me. What's going on? Did you get the letter?"

"What letter? I'm not at the office. In fact, I'm at your home."

"My home? Why?"

"Your alarm system went off. It's okay. No one got in, but we'll need you to come by so we can check out inside."

She rose, her feet taking her towards Jonah. "Just let me tell Jonah I'm heading home and I'll be on my way."

"Candace, bring Jonah with you. Don't come on your own." The call ended abruptly as Candace stared at her phone.

"Candace?" Jonah's voice beside her caused her to jump.

"Jonah. I have to go home. Someone tried to break in. That was Bill. He wants you to go with me."

"That's not why you're out here though." He pushed back the cap he was wearing, staring at his muddy hands and clothes. "Let me get cleaned up and we'll head in. Leave your car here for now."

She stared at him, wondering why he said that.

"You're not in any condition to drive right now. Bill has you scared." He pointed towards the house. "Come, sit on the deck. I won't be long."

Candace stared at the flashing blue and red lights from the emergency vehicles parked outside her home as Jonah parked and withdrew the key from the ignition. His eyes on her, he waited for her to speak. When she didn't, he reached to lay a hand on her arm, drawing it back when she jumped.

"Let's go see what they've found, Candace. And then you can tell me why you came to find me. Sit tight. I'll get your door."

Candace's hand grasped Jonah's tight as they walked towards Bill, who turned as they approached, an inscrutable look on his face.

"Bill?"

"Can we have your keys, Candace, and the code to the alarm?   I want my officers to go through your house before we talk."

She handed him her keys as well as muttering the security code.   What next, Lord? she thought.   Who did this?   Jonah stood beside her, his heart too in prayer, her hand tight in his once more.

Bill returned, handing her the keys.

"It's clear inside, Candace.   They didn't make it in, although they certainly had time to.   Whoever set up your security system is good."

She gave a half smile.   "You can thank my cousin's husband's security team for that."   She missed the look Bill shot her before looking at Jonah.

Candace stopped at the entry of her home, drawing a deep breath, before entering.   A puzzled look on her face, she wandered through the rooms, finally stopping in her office, looking around.

"Someone's been in here, Bill."

"They have? But your doors were locked."

She nodded. "I know, but there has been someone here." She moved towards the filing cabinet, pulling it open, then jumping back, a small scream coming from her.

Bill was at her side, staring into the open drawer. "This is not yours, I take it, and shouldn't be here."

Candace stared down at the bloody knife. "It looks as if it could have come from the kitchen but I can't be certain. And I certainly didn't place it there." She turned, her face pale and walked into Jonah's arms.

"Get her out of here, Jonah. We need to work this scene." Bill watched Jonah lead Candace away. "And Jonah, find out who installed her system."

"Try Abe Findlay from Riverville. Two of his guys did. Emma, her cousin, is married to Abe."

Bill spun back around at the names and groaned. There was no way this should have happened, he thought, pulling out his phone to make that call to Andrew he had been dreading.

Back at Jonah's, Candace paced his living room, her face still pale. Jonah watched as Rusty paced right along with her, his muzzle tilted up to watch her face, his side brushing along her leg at every step.

"Who would do that, Jonah?"

"I don't know, Candace. They're working on it."

"First my business, now my home." She groaned. "Abe's going to come take me to his security compound, lock it up tight, and throw away the key. I just know he is."

Jonah grinned at that. "I don't think so. I won't let him take you away."

She stopped, then turned slowly to watch him. "You won't?" When he shook his head, she spoke. "Then, this makes it even worse. I was out here today to tell you I got another note. This time with a picture. A picture of you. They've threatened you, Jonah."

“Threatened me? How?”

“If you don’t stay away from me, they’ve threatened to harm you. I don’t know how, they didn’t say.”

“It doesn’t matter, Candace. I’m not staying away from you.” Jonah walked towards her, stopping as she backed away. “Your friendship means too much to me. You too. I’ll not let anyone come between us.” He watched for a reaction but saw none. “Now, tell me. Why would Abe lock you up?”

She shrugged. “Emma must have told him something. Ian and Murphy just didn’t happen by the other day. They were here for a purpose, one of which was that security system.” She stopped and groaned. “I need to call Abe and let him know someone got in.”

“I would say someone had already planned this. They knew exactly where to leave the knife.” He paused as a knock came to his door.

“Bill, hi. Come on in. What news do you have?”

A sober look was on his face. "It's not good, Jonah. Candace, did you ever notice one of your knives from the business kitchen missing?"

She spun, staring at him. "They were all there on the Saturday when Emma and Abe were through the building. Emma commented on them, wanting to know what brand they were. I wasn't back through until Monday morning. Why?"

"Because it's one of the knives from your kitchen. We looked at the photos the crime scene techs took and it's the missing one."

"And you're just now telling me a knife was missing from my kitchen? And that it was planted to frame me?" Candace was furious. "You know what? If you want any more information from me, call my lawyer. I'm done with the insinuations."

She ran from the house and the men heard her car speeding away.

Bill sighed. "That's not how I wanted to ask her."

Jonah nodded. "No, it's not how it should have gone. Now fix it, Bill." He stared at his friend. "Something's going on with you, Bill. What is it?"

Bill stood, his eyes raised to the ceiling as if in prayer before he finally nodded. "Three months ago, I got word that Mom has cancer, Stage III breast. She's under treatment right now, but the surgeon doesn't think he got it all."

Jonah stood frozen. "Why are you still working then? Shouldn't you be with her?"

Bill nodded. "I asked to be with her. She sent me and my siblings away. She's...." Bill's voice died away. "I can't explain it, Jonah, but it's like she's in denial and doesn't want us to see how much she's hurting. Dad keeps us updated but it's not the same."

"Listen, Bill. Have you talked to Andrew at all? You need to be there, regardless of what she has said."

Bill nodded, his eyes on the floor. "I know, but how do I do that when she was so specific." He paused, pulling out his phone. "It's my Dad." He listened for a while, asked a few questions, then stared at the phone before dialling a number. "Andrew?

That time I asked for? I need to leave in the morning but I'm standing here with Jonah trying to figure out where to go with the investigation involving Candace. What's that? A letter and a photo? No, I haven't been in the office. Okay, I'll be there shortly. The thing of it is, we may need to bring in protection for her at some point."

Jonah watched as Bill drew a deep breath. "Go, be with your family, Bill. Our prayers are with you. Now, I need to go find Candace."

Bill nodded as Jonah followed him out. "I'm sorry about tonight, Jonah."

Jonah shrugged. "She's running, Bill, from what I have no idea. I don't think she does either, to tell you the truth. Whoever takes over for you needs to talk to her cousin, Emma."

"Emma?" Bill stopped for a moment.

"Emma Findlay.   Tell them to call Trackers."

Bill shot him a look that Jonah ignored. Now where is she, Lord? I need to find this lady before she gets hurt.

Jonah watched the taillights of Bill's car fade down the lane, then sighed, turning to his own vehicle. Where would Candace go to? He drove through town, finally ending up at her home, where he exited the vehicle and stood, watching the activity still going on. He turned and saw her, standing by herself under the neighbour's tree. He walked towards her, not quite sure how to proceed.

"Why did they do that, Jonah?" Candace's quiet question whispered through the night air to him.

He stopped beside her. "I have no idea, but we'll get it figured out. Bill wanted me to apologize for him. He's heading out of town tomorrow morning. His mother's fighting cancer and that's been affecting him."

She nodded. "I understand. But where do I go from here? I can't be around you."

Andrew spoke from in front of her, causing her to jump. "It won't matter any more, Candace. If you're not together, they'll still go after Jonah to draw you out. And being here is not smart."

She nodded. "I know. I was just hoping I could go home."

"You can't. Not likely for a day or so. Jonah, can you walk her over to my place? Phoebe's expecting her."

Candace shook her head. "I can't do that, Andrew."

"You can and you will. Phoebe's expecting you to come. Jonah?"

"I'll make sure she gets there. No chance of getting anything out of the house?"

Andrew shook his head. "Not tonight."

Chapter 8

Phoebe turned the next morning and watched as Candace approached the kitchen.

"Good morning. How'd you sleep?"

Candace shrugged. "Not that great. Thanks for letting me stay." She pulled a chair back and sat. "Has Andrew been around and said when I can go home?"

Phoebe shook her head. "He hasn't been home yet, but should be shortly."

"I'm sorry, Phoebe?"

"Sorry for what? Andrew's working."

"I know, but maybe he wouldn't be if it weren't for me."

Phoebe shook her head as she handed Candace a cup of tea. "It's who he is, Candace. With Bill away, he'll be picking up more."

Candace stared at her cup, not raising her head as she heard voices behind her. The chair sliding out beside her didn't even register. She jumped as a hand touched hers, looking up to see Jonah watching her.

"Candace?"

"Jonah, you need to stop looking after me. You have work you need to be doing." She rose and almost ran from the room.

Jonah's head dropped as he listened to her footsteps receding. Andrew and Phoebe shared a glance, then Andrew sat, drawing Jonah's attention.

"What do I do, Andrew?"

"Just keep what you're doing, being her friend. She's struggling with a lot right now. I spoke with Emma. Abe does want her to come their way, but his team has just left on an assignment. She wasn't too sure how long it would last."

"So where does that leave us?"

"Solving this as soon as we can. I'll need her to come into the department today to give a statement. Bill said she didn't want to talk to him last night."

"No, she didn't. For some reason, she got really hostile and threatened not to talk without her lawyer present."

Andrew drew a deep breath. "That might be a good idea, Jonah. Does she have one?"

"I don't know. I'll find out and if she doesn't, then Lee from the church would likely step in."

"Call him and have him meet you at the department. She should have representation."

Candace turned from where she stood on the front porch as Jonah approached her. Her eyes were shuttered, her face closed.

"Come on, Candace. Let me take you to the department."

"Am I under arrest?"

He shook his head. "No. Andrew just wants to get a statement from you. But he has asked if you have a lawyer."

She shook her head. "Not for something like this."

"Then, let me call Lee Simons from church. He'll meet us there."

She sighed. "More money I need to come up with." She stomped down the few steps to Jonah's car.

Jonah held the door for her. "It's not official, Candace. This is for your protection as much as anything."

She gave an abrupt nod, then looked down. She sighed again. "Why, Jonah? What did I ever do to deserve this?"

"It's nothing you've done, Candace. It's what someone's done to you. Now, do you need to stop anywhere?"

"Yes, I do. I want to stop at my home and my business."

"Sorry, love. We can't stop at your home but we can see if we can stop at your business. Something there you need?"

She nodded. "I need a change of clothes. I think I had some at the business, but now I'm not so sure."

"Tell you what. I know Grace from the store downtown will open up for you to get something and let you change there. Let me call her."

She sighed and he heard her muttering about owing someone else. He bit back a grin at the disgruntled tone in her voice.

An hour later, she sat in an interrogation room at the department, waiting for someone to take her statement. She looked up at the gray-haired man who stopped in the doorway.

"You must be Candace Owens. I'm Lee Simons. Jonah seemed to think you needed my help."

"Yes, he does seem to think that. I have no idea why."

"Let's talk. Lily said someone would be here soon to take a statement from you. Tell me what all has been happening."

Lee listened as she spoke, taking notes, asking questions as needed. He finally sat back, his eyes on her face.

"There's nothing to worry about, Candace. This is just a formality today. Andrew knows that as well."

"But what about the knife?"

"What about it? Your fingerprints will be on it if it is the missing one. The security system will log when the system went off."

She nodded, not quite sure she felt any better. Her eyes lifted as Lily stopped in the doorway. "You're ready for my statement, Lily?"

"I am. And it's fine if Lee wants to stay."

Lee nodded. "I think I will, if Candace wants."

"I do want. Thank you."

Two hours later, Jonah looked up from the field he was working in to see Candace walking towards him.

"Candace? Why are you here? Don't you have meals to make?"

"I do but Ev took over today. I think she's enjoying that. She told me she had never thought of doing something like what I do. I'll have to be careful or she'll steal my clients."

"Never but she might be interested into going to partnership with you, knowing Ev."

"A partnership? Why?"

Jonah shrugged. "It's what she does. She's done it before. Now, how did it go today?"

She bent to the tomato plants, searching for the ripe ones and picking them, gently placing them in the baskets he had ready. "All right, I suppose. Lee Simons was there. He doesn't think I have anything to worry about."

"No, I don't think you do either. Listen, Emma called me."

"Emma? Great! She's meddling now."

Jonah broke out into laughter. "Is that what you call it?"

She nodded. "She is. If it wasn't her, it would be one of the guys."

Jonah kept laughing, causing Candace to turn outraged eyes at him. "You think that's funny? Trust me. You don't want those eight guys, plus a couple of others, providing security for you. You would have no life."

Jonah's hands went up in the air as he tried to curb his laughter, without success. "Yeah, they are sort of intimidating."

"No sort of about it. When you see them in their dark blue uniforms with their guns and frowns in place, they are." She looked around the field. "Now, what else is there to do?"

"This is actually the last of it for today." He reached to lift the baskets to the wagon. "Do you want to drive?"

She looked at the tractor and shook her head. "I'll walk, thank you very much."

He laughed again. "I'll meet you at the house then. Rusty's around somewhere. He'll be happy to see you."

Jonah watched as Candace pushed with her toes to start the porch swing, Rusty curled up beside her, his chin on her knee. He sank into one of the rockers.

"So, how did it really go?"

She shrugged, her eyes to the distance. "Okay, I guess. I still feel like I'm a suspect."

"Trust me. If you were a true suspect, they would have told you."

"I guess." She turned to Jonah. "I still think you should stay away from me."

"Not happening. Now, I'm heading in to clean up, then I'm taking you to dinner."

She shook her head. "I don't think so."

"I am. I owe you a meal or two. Have they released your home yet?"

She shook her head. "Not yet. They think by tomorrow. That means I have to find somewhere to stay tonight."

"Andrew's?"

She shook her head. "They're off somewhere overnight and tomorrow." She sighed. "I guess it's the bed and breakfast for me."

"Not so fast. Andrew's mother volunteered to have you stay. Take her up on it."

She stared at him. "Why are they being so nice?"

"Because that's who they are and what they do. It's Biblical, you know, to show hospitality."

❧ ❧ ❧ ❧

Saturday afternoon, Candace walked through her home, searching for what she wasn't sure. Then she realized something was missing. She spun to stare at the mantle. That's it, she thought. They took the picture of Emma and me. But why? She almost ran to her purse, fumbling for her phone.

"Emma? They took that picture of us."

"The one from last summer?"

Candace could feel the fear coursing through her body. "That one. You need to be careful."

"Abe's home. I'll talk to him. Candace, we need to do something about you."

"No. I think I'm safe for now. Andrew said he had a team he would call in if needed. I can't have you or Abe close to me. You need to think of your son."

Emma sighed. "That I do and I know Abe won't be happy you're staying away like this."

"I have to, Emma. I don't want you dragged into this." She sighed as she heard the doorbell. "But then you already are.

Listen, I have someone at my door. Call me later?"

"I will. Let me talk to Abe and we'll see what we can come up with."

Candace stood for a moment, hand flat on the door, her heart racing. She wasn't expecting anyone. Peeking out the window, she frowned at the ladies standing there, around her own age, she thought. Phoebe was with them.

Opening the door, Candace looked to Phoebe for answers.

"Candace. Hi! Can we come in?" Phoebe's eyes sparkled with mirth.

Candace smiled at her. "Off course you can. What am I thinking?" She stepped back. "Sorry, it's a bit of a mess. I was at the market this morning and haven't been able to do my normal cleaning."

"From what I hear, there's not much left for you to clean. I'm Julia. This is Paige, Aideen, Faith, and Larkin. We're all married to friends of Jonah."

"He mentioned something about you ladies stopping by. Thank you. Now what can I get you?"

"We're not here to be social, Candace." Aideen groaned as the women laughed. "That didn't come out right. We're off for a shopping trip in Oak City and want you to join us. The mall is open late."

Candace stared at them, then shrugged. "It beats cleaning, I guess. Do I need to change?"

They all shook their head.

"No, just grab your purse and lock up." Phoebe spoke up. "And show me your security system. Andrew's jealous."

Candace started to laugh. "It's way more than what I need, I can tell you that. Abe went overboard. He seemed to think he needed to."

Questioning looks made her explain, and the ladies laughed as they sorted themselves out into the vehicle.

❦ ❦ ❦ ❦

Candace settled back on her deck chair late that night, phone to her ear. Jonah had called earlier that afternoon and she hadn't had a chance to call him. Getting only his voice mail, she sighed and then shut off her phone. She really needed some God time on her own. She searched her phone for the right app and then started reading. Peace once more flowed through her. She didn't hear the steps on the grass until she saw the dark form rise in front of her. A hand over her mouth kept her from screaming and then she was bundled into arms and then into a car. Blindfolded and gagged, her hands bound, she had no idea where she was headed. Her phone lay on the deck, ringing with the tone she had programmed in for Jonah.

Chapter 9

Jonah paced outside the church the next morning, his eyes watching for Candace. Andrew and Phoebe shared a look before they stopped near him.

"Jonah?"

He spun as he heard his name called. "Andrew! Did either one of you talk to Candace this morning?"

Phoebe shook her head. "The ladies and I dropped her off early yesterday evening. I haven't spoken to her since. Why?"

"She called late last night, but didn't leave a message. I haven't been able to reach her at all."

Andrew's face grew stern. "We need to go check on that. Phoebe?"

"I'll wait in the truck for you, Andrew. Now let's go."

Jonah rang the doorbell once again, with no response. Andrew studied the house and then walked around to the back deck. He froze, seeing Candace's phone on the deck. Then, he moved to the door, testing it. Opening it, he walked through, not finding her. Sighing, he reached for his phone as he walked back out and around to the front, finding Jonah heading his way.

"Andrew?"   Jonah stopped with Andrew held up a hand and spoke into his phone.

Andrew slipped the phone back into his pocket. "She's not here, Jonah. Her car is. Her purse is. Her phone is on the back deck. But she's not around."

Jonah froze.   "They've taken her then?"

Andrew nodded. "We need to move back from here and let the officers do their thing."   His eyes connected with Phoebe. "We'll find her for you, Jonah."

Jonah nodded, not catching the words Andrew spoke until he walked away. Then he spun to stare at him before heading after him.

The responding officers shook their head and one spoke.

"It's like she vanished into thin air, Chief. No signs of any struggle. Nothing."

"I didn't think there would be. Thanks."

Jonah had been watching Andrew's face and nodded when he approached him.

"No sign of anything right?"

Andrew shook his head. "No. She's just vanished." He groaned as his phone chimed and he looked at it. "And it's her cousin. Has she been trying to reach you?"

Jonah pulled out his phone and nodded. "She has. She says something about a picture of Candace and Emma being missing and that Candace called her about 9:30 last night." Jonah raised his eyes. "Why take that picture?"

Andrew shrugged. "It more than likely is to throw us off the investigation." He turned. "Listen, Jonah, head for home. Stay safe. I'll call you later with an update."

Jonah hesitated before nodding and heading for his vehicle. Now what, Lord? Where is she? Keep her safe.

❦ ❦ ❦ ❦

Three days later, Jonah paused at the park in town, his brow furrowed as he struggled to make sense of what was happening. He walked further towards the river, not hearing the two men who approached him from behind. He stopped, leaning on the railing, just watching the water flow pass.

"Jonah, don't turn around."

He straightened, frowning. He should know that voice. "I won't but where is Candace?"

"We don't know that. That's not why we're here. We need your help."

Jonah snorted. "Unless you know where Candace is, I have nothing to offer."

"Just listen to us." The second man spoke, shooting a glance behind him at the third man standing in the shadows. "You've lived in this town all your life. Right now, there are illegal practices going on. You have certified organics on your farm, we know that. There are others here who have obtained that fraudulently. We need your help to expose them."

"And how do I do that?" Jonah stiffened, finally understanding what they were saying. "And this illegal stuff? They're using chemicals that will harm or kill?"

"You do understand. Find out what you can and help us to clean that up."

He waited for something more to be said before turning. The men had gone. The third man had stepped back into the shadows, watchful, before he pulled off his hoodie and straightened his cap. He needed to be off before Jonah saw him.

Jonah searched the area, then sighed. What more could be added to his plate, he wondered? Lord, I just can't do this any more on my own. This is where You come in, I guess.

He turned, tracing his steps back to his vehicle, his eyes on the police department. Then, he shook his head. No, he didn't have enough information to go there. No, he didn't have any information. He needed to go home and do his research. He had a good idea of which farmers he had been warned about.

He watched the pedestrians as he headed home, not sure who it was he was even searching for. He frowned. He knew the voices, he just couldn't put a name to them.

Now how did he do what they wanted? And how did it, if it did, tie to Candace? He shrugged his shoulders as he drove towards his home, his thoughts racing as he tried to understand what was going on.

His phone chimed as he climbed the steps to his door and he paused, squinting in the sun to see who it was.

"Andrew? Tell me you have word."

"Sorry, Jonah. I don't, not about Candace. But something else has come up and I need your input. Can we meet?"

Jonah paced back down the stairs and looked towards his produce. "I have a lot of work to do in the fields today, Andrew. I just got back from a trip to town."

"That's okay. I'm heading your way late this afternoon. That should work."

"Bring Phoebe and I'll treat you to some home-grown produce."

"Now, that sounds like a plan. I'm pretty sure she's free."

Jonah headed for his fields, Rusty at his side, but his mind was elsewhere. *Where are you, Candace? Are you safe? And what have we gotten into?*

He sighed as his phone chimed with a text message. At this rate, he'd get nothing done today. His eyes read the message even as his heart sank. Whoever had Candace wanted something from him and they'd be in touch. What did he have that they'd want?

❧ ❧ ❧ ❧

Andrew wiped his hands on his napkin and pushed his plate away before sitting back in his chair, his eyes looking over the land around him.

"That was delicious, Jonah. What kind of vinaigrette did you use?" Phoebe's quiet questions during the meal had helped to keep the balance for them.

Andrew listened to their conversations, his mind on what he needed to talk to Jonah about.

Finally, Jonah turned to Andrew. "You wanted to talk?"

"I did, but I'm not sure how to go about it."

"Just say what you have to say." Jonah's eyes never left Andrew's face.

"Well, then, here goes. The body in the freezer belongs to an agricultural inspector who went missing a couple of weeks ago. How he ended up there, we have no idea. We're working on tracking his steps. He wasn't knived but the bloody knife Candace found is from her kitchen. It was animal blood on it."

"Animal blood?" Jonah shot a look at Phoebe. "You're okay with this, Phoebe?"

She nodded. "I'm fine with it, Jonah. Let Andrew continue."

"Now to the letters and threats. They seem aimless, not coordinated at all. It's like more than one person is writing them without knowing what the other is saying."

"Is it to scare her?"

Andrew nodded. "It could be. It could also be to drive her away from town. She's adamant that she only sources organic produce and meats. Some of the traditional farmers and growers have not been happy with that, but she doesn't have a large enough volume to warrant them taking any steps against her."

Jonah sighed. "Then, what happened today makes sense."

Andrew frowned. "What happened today?"

Jonah told him about his conversation with the two men and what they wanted from him.

"Falsified documentation? That can happen?"

Jonah nodded. "It can and from what I understand, it can be into a lot of money if they play their cards right. I'm working through this, trying to think of who it might be." He pulled out his phone. "Then I got this after I talked with you."

Andrew took Jonah's phone as he shared a look with Phoebe. He didn't like what he was hearing. He read the text, then sent it to his own phone.

"What they are asking of you is highly irregular, you know."

Jonah nodded. "I don't have that kind of information or even access to it. How would I? I'm not in government. I don't make the rules of how organic farms run. Are these two tied together somehow?"

Andrew nodded. "I think they are. I'll have one of our people look into this for us. In the meantime, we need you to stay safe. How do we do that?"

"I'm not running away, Andrew. I have too much to do here. I have people dependent on my supplying their needs with the produce."

Andrew nodded. "So, do you need any help?"

Jonah sat back, his eyes on his friend before they moved to Phoebe, who nodded. "I could always use some help, particularly at this time of year. Why?"

"Let me work on that for you, then. Phoebe, we should run. It's getting late and you have an early day tomorrow."

She rose and hugged Jonah. "That I do. Jonah, we're praying for both you and Candace."

"Thank you.   It's appreciated.   I wonder, if all this is God's way of showing Candace how much He loves her." He left it at that, but Andrew and Phoebe studied him before looking at each other.

Chapter 10

$\mathcal{A}$ week later, Andrew searched for Bill, asking some questions before sending him Jonah's way.   He turned back to his office, a frown on his face.   He wanted to know where Candace was but had no idea. It was almost two weeks since she disappeared.   He prayed she was safe and unharmed.

Bill found Jonah in the farthest greenhouse on his farm, having been sent that way by the officer working with Jonah. Andrew had assigned one of the patrol officer to work with Jonah during the week.

"Jonah? Got a moment?"

Jonah looked around the plants he was working on.   "Sure.   Just give me a few minutes to finish with these."

"What on earth are you doing to them? Bill stared at the leaves on the ground.

"I remove what we call sucker vines from these tomatoes. They grow better if you strip them."

Bill shook his head. "I'm glad that's you doing this and not me."

Finally, Jonah straightened up and looked at his hands. "Let me wash up and then I'll go find us some coffee. Leslie should be ready for some too."

"Actually, I need to talk to you without Leslie around."

Jonah stopped, his eyes on Bill. "Okay." He drew the word out. "Let me get him some anyway. He likes to have his while relaxing in the hammock near the back of the yard."

Bill finally set his mug down and leaned forward on his arms. "Andrew sent me out. He wanted to know how you were doing."

"And he couldn't ask himself."

Bill shook his head. "For some reason, he thinks he's being watched and it has to do with you and Candace. He didn't say why."

"I don't like that, Bill. Why would someone be watching him?"

Bill shrugged. "I have no idea. But he did say he'd been working on finding out who you could talk to about the organics problem." He held up his hands. "He's had me working on that as well, in-between other things."

Jonah sat, silenced for the moment. "I'm not sure I can do anything, Bill, no matter who Andrew digs up for me to talk to.   I have no proof and without proof nothing can be done."

Bill nodded. "We know that. That website Josiah set up months ago? It's still generating leads and apparently there's something on there about this. I'll have him send it to you."

Jonah nodded as he sat back, turning his cup in his hands, his mind not on what they had been talking about. "Any word on Candace?"

Bill shook his head. "There hasn't been. Ev and Avery are working with her clients and keeping that going. Ev said she's picked up even more clients for Candace, but they understand Candace has to talk to them and then decide on what they would actually need. For now, Ev supplying what she can, working from Candace's notes and recipes."

"Candace is not here and her business is growing. I hope it doesn't outgrow her."

"There's no danger of that. Ev has people lined up who want to work with her."

Jonah was silent again, his heart raised in prayer for the lady he knew he was beginning to love. Lord, I have no idea where she is but You do. Bring her home safe, please Lord. I know she's struggled with understanding Your love for her. Touch her in a special way, please, Dear Lord.

Bill finally walked away, after having watched Jonah head back to work. A thought was niggling at him, and he wanted to work it through before he talked to Andrew. He knew who he needed to talk to and headed towards the church and Silas.

❧ ❧ ❧ ❧

Candace stood at the window of the room she was locked in, her hands pressing against the glass as she studied the yard around the house. She knew the window was nailed shut. She had tried many times to open it. She couldn't budge it. There was no window in the small bathroom attached to the room. The only door was locked at all the times. She was forced to stand with her back to it when her meals were brought it. Threats had been made against her if she didn't. She felt the bruising on her arms and face from when she hadn't done what they asked of her.

She had no idea what they wanted from her. They hadn't said. They seemed to be waiting for something. She sighed and laid her head again the window pane, her eyes closing as tears slid down her face. She prayed and prayed for release that didn't come. She wasn't sure how long she had been there. Days seemed to run into one another.

She stiffened as she heard the lock click open behind her. She didn't turn as she heard footsteps approaching her and jumped when a blindfold was wrapped over her eyes. A hand on her arm forced her forward. She struggled to get loose but the hand tightened and she heard the threats again, threats against Emma and against Jonah. Lord, please keep me safe. Help me to say alive.

Candace was shoved down stairs and then into a chair, blindfold in place. She couldn't stop the tears, the tears of pain, frustration, anger, fear. She saw the light focused on her under the edges of her blindfold, that is, until it was removed. She tried to raise her hand to block the light but her hands were held tight behind her. She didn't understand. She wasn't given anything to say, nor was she asked to hold anything. A twist on her wrist had her giving a cry of pain and fresh tears fell. After a few moments, she was blindfolded once again and dragged up the stairs, back to her prison. Lord, why? Why hasn't someone found me already? I don't want to die here but if I do, make sure my family knows I love them.

She sank down onto the pile of blankets they had provided her, finding one to cover herself with. Her eyes closed, she slept, tears still trickling down her face in her sleep. She didn't hear the door unlock or the footsteps that stopped at her side. The man looked at her for a moment, raised his eyes to the window, and sighed. Somehow, he needed to get her out of there or get word to someone where she was being held. But how?

❦ ❦ ❦ ❦

Jonah groaned in the predawn light as his phone chimed with a text message. Who was it at this time of the day? He rolled over, reaching for his phone, his hand freezing in place as he saw the text message and then the video sent separately. Candace! He needed to talk to Andrew but had been warned not to. He was torn, wanting to do what was right, but not wanting to harm Candace any more than she was already.

He reached for his clothes, dressing rapidly, and almost ran for his truck, letting Rusty out at the same time. He knew Leslie would be there soon, but he knew what needed to be done. He had confessed to Jonah that if Jonah really needed someone to work for him, he was willing to quit the force and do just that.

Jonah's hands shook as he headed into town, his eyes searching for someone watching him leave. He prayed as he hadn't in a long time.

Andrew stood in his doorway, a cup of coffee in hand, as he saw Jonah walking towards him. He hadn't had much sleep last night but that seemed to be becoming his norm.

"Jonah? It's really early, you know." Andrew pointed at the kitchen chair and then handed him a cup of coffee. "Can I get you breakfast?"

Jonah looked up, suddenly realizing how early it was. "I'm sorry, Andrew. I didn't think about the time. I hope I didn't wake you."

"No, I was up anyway. I have some meetings early this morning. But why are you here?" His eyes searched his friend's face, seeing new lines in it.

Jonah handed him his phone. "This is why."

Andrew once more searched Jonah's face before he turned to the phone. His face tightened at the text message and grew even sterner at the video.

"This is brutal, Jonah."

"It is, Andrew. How do we find her? And what exactly do they want?"

Andrew shook his head. "I need your phone for the day. Is that possible?"

Jonah nodded. "Take it. See what you can come up with." He froze as it chimed with another text message. Reaching for it, he read.

"What's this, Andrew? Who is this?"

Andrew reached for the phone again. "Someone knows where she is? Just great. My ETF team is away for the day training." He stood and paced, his thoughts racing before he pulled out his phone.

"Richard. Andrew. I didn't get you up, did I?" Andrew listened for a moment then spoke once more. "I need your team's help. How soon can you be here? An hour? Yeah, that works."

Andrew spun to Jonah. "I'm canceling my meetings this morning. Richard and his team will be here. Once I find out where she is, they'll go in and get her."

Jonah nodded, his mind whirling. What had just happened? His phone chimed again, this time with an address. Wordlessly, he held it out to Andrew.

Phoebe appeared in the doorway, took one look and headed to make fresh coffee and then their breakfast. She knew it would be a long day for them. She finally had to leave, catching Andrew for a few words. She smiled at Richard and his team as the entered, heading for the kitchen.

"Andrew? What do we have?" Richard stopped by the coffee pot, pouring coffee for them all.

"We just got an address. Someone with the kidnappers is letting us know what is happening."

"Has to be someone undercover then. Okay, so now what?"

Plans were made and discarded. Andrew was on the phone in between the discussions, ensuring his officers were up to date on what was happening.

Richard finally sat back in the early afternoon sunlight. "I think that's about as best as we can do, Andrew. We don't know how many we'll find there."

Andrew nodded. "I'll let your team run it, but keep me in the loop." He looked at Jonah, who sat slumped in his chair, head in his hands. "Let's pray first, people, then we move."

Richard nodded. "Let's do that. We can't do this on our own, that's for sure."

Chapter 11

$\mathcal{R}$ichard studied the building in front of them. It was a solid brick house, two stories, but looked as if it hadn't been a home for years. That is, until he looked at the driveway and saw the tire tracks crushing the weeds. He pointed to his four teams members and three of them silently headed for the side and back yards. Silver stayed with him. He wanted one of the ladies on his team with him when he went in.

Richard's hand reached for the door knob, turning it slowly. Good, he thought, it's unlocked. Let's hope it doesn't squeak. Silver crept in the house behind him, their eyes searching. They heard the snores before they found the guard. Moving quickly, Richard had him disarmed and on the floor, handcuffed.

"Move wrong, and this lady will deal with you."   Richard's voice was a low growl.

The young man nodded, fright now apparent in his eyes. He had failed, hadn't he? He watched as Richard moved silently through the house, searching the downstairs before heading up the elaborate staircase to the second floor. He searched, finding the only room that was locked. He reached with the keys he had taken from the guard, unlocking the door, yet hesitating to open it. What would he find on the other side?

With weapon in one hand, he reached and gently shoved the door open, his eyes searching the room before finding Candace huddled on the blankets, not moving. He holstered his weapon and moved forward, crouching to feel for a pulse. His eyes raised, he drew a breath of relief. He quickly scooped her up and headed back down the stairs, with a quick motion of his head sending Silver and her captive out the door. He swung the door closed behind him and paced quickly to the vehicle, sliding Candace onto one of the seats and then seating himself beside her. Stephen sat on her other side, and as the paramedic on the team, already assessing her. He raised his eyes to Richard, shaking his head.

Richard sighed. He prayed that she hadn't been hurt too badly and that she could help identify who took her but he knew that was a stretch. He reached for his phone, even as he kept an arm around Candace to steady her against the vehicle movements.

"Andrew? We have the package. We're heading your way."

"Good. I'll be here. Do we need anyone else?"

"We might. Stephen will let us know." He pocketed his phone, his eyes searching all around as his head kept in constant motion.

"No one's following us, Richard." Silver spoke from the seat in front of him. "What are we to do with him?"

"Andrew can have him. I'm sure he'll have plenty of questions to ask." Richard grave a grim smile as the captive guard shook his head.

"He'll kill me, even behind bars." There was panic in the voice.

"That's something you should have thought of before, buddy."

Jonah stood just inside the door of Andrew's house, watching as Richard carried Candace in, his eyes raised and watchful that he didn't hit her head or legs. Andrew pointed to their spare room and Richard headed that way, Stephen and Naomi at his heels.

Andrew turned to Silver. "He fight you much?"

She started to laugh, bringing eyes to her face. "He didn't fight at all. Richard got the drop on him. He was sleeping, if you can believe that."

Andrew nodded. "That was helpful, wasn't it? I have Bill on his way over with an escort. He'll question him back at the department. He hasn't asked for a lawyer yet?"

Silver shook her head. "No, he hasn't. But then we haven't asked him anything much yet. Listen, do you have coffee?"

"There's coffee and Phoebe was back through with some food. Ev sent it over. It's in the kitchen for you." He turned to speak with Jonah and stopped, his eyes on his friend's face.

Jonah's eyes were glued to the door behind which Candace lay. He barely felt Richard's hands on his shoulders, pushing him down into a chair, handing him food and coffee. He didn't hear Andrew telling him to eat. They finally took the plate of food and cup from him, knowing he wouldn't eat.

Stephen finally came out, his brow furrowed, and headed for the kitchen. He spoke a few quiet words to Andrew and Richard before turning to search for Jonah. Jonah had risen and now stood in the kitchen door. The guard Richard's team had captured was gone, taken to the department for questioning. Andrew had given strict instructions about his safety and prayed that it would be enough.

Jonah stood silent for a moment, his eyes on Stephen.

"Stephen? Candace? How is she?"

"She's battered some, Jonah, and dehydrated. I'm heading out to our office and grabbing some supplies. I want to start an IV. I've been in touch with a physician I trust and she'll be out here if I need her to. Right now, she's been awake and is sleeping. Naomi's with her, just to watch. Give us a bit and I'll let you in to see her." Stephen watched as Jonah's eyes slid shut, before sharing a long look with Andrew and Richard. "Right now, what you can do for her is have something to eat. We need you to keep up your strength."

Jonah nodded, then sank into one of the kitchen chairs. Richard once more set a bowl of soup in front of him.

"Eat, Jonah. Even if it's only that bowl of soup. Do you need to head back to your place for anything?"

Jonah shook his head. "No. Leslie has it under control. Andrew, don't be surprised if he resigns to come work for me. He says he enjoys it much more than being a beat officer as he puts it."

Andrew paused, cup halfway to his mouth, then laughed. "Somehow that doesn't surprise me. He's always reading these agriculture magazines and trying to grow stuff in his apartment. Good stuff, that is."

Richard laughed as well. "Now, what more can we do, Andrew? If nothing else, then I'll take Timothy and Silver and head out. Stephen will be here for a while now that's he's back with his supplies. Naomi has offered to stay for a while."

"No, I think we're good. Thank you, Richard, for what you did." He paused as Jonah's phone rang.

Jonah reached for it, his eyes blurring as he read the number, then answered it. "Abe? I thought it would be Emma calling."

"She wanted to but she's putting our little guy to bed. Tell me you have good news."

"We do. Richard went in and found her and brought her to Andrew." Jonah could hear the sigh of relief from the other end of the phone. "She's sleeping right now. Call me again tomorrow or the next day, or call Andrew and we'll bring you up to date on what's gone on."

"Thank you for the good news, Jonah. Em will sleep better tonight."

Richard watched, a puzzled look on his face, that Andrew caught.

"Abe Findlay's wife, Emma? You know her?" When Richard nodded, Andrew continued. "Emma and Candace are cousins."

Richard finally nodded. "I'm surprised you didn't call in Abe and his team."

"I wanted someone local here, who knew the area. Abe's not familiar with our town. You are. Don would have been my next call, but he's more familiar with Oak City."

Richard nodded again. "That's true. Listen, now that's Stephen back, I'm heading out. Call me if you need to."

❧ ❧ ❧ ❧

Candace slowly roused, her ears listening for the footsteps that always meant something was going to happen. She heard nothing. She turned, feeling a pull on one hand. She frowned, not understanding how the blankets could feel so soft. Her eyes opened slowly and she searched the room, a frown in place. She knew this room. She had stayed here. Why was she here and how did she get here? This was Andrew and Phoebe's place.

As she moved, she felt the pull again on her hand and looked. An IV? What was going on? She heard the sound of the door cracking open and shot a glance that way. She didn't recognize the man who stood there for a moment, and who then walked in on quiet feet around the bed to check her IV.

"Good morning. I'm Stephen. Don't worry, you're safe. We got you out two days ago."

"Two days?" Her voice was hoarse and Stephen bent to help her drink. "I'm at Andrew's?"

"You are. We felt you were safer here. Don't worry, again. I think I'm repeating myself." A grin split the dark brown beard he sported. "We've had a physician here to see you. We can pull the IV today and get you started on liquids."

"Jonah? Is he safe? They wanted him. Wanted to trade me for me or something like that." Lines furrowed her brow as she tried to remember.

"Hey. None of that right now. That can come later. Right now, we need to focus on getting you up and on your feet. One of my team members, Naomi, is here as well.

138

She can help you if you want to clean up some."

He turned to walk away, turning as she spoke.

"Thank you, Stephen. I have no idea who you are or what team you're talking about, but if it wasn't for you, I wouldn't have made it out."

He shrugged. "It's what we do, Candace. I hear tell that you're related to Abe. We do what he does."

Candace's mouth fell open in surprise as he grinned again and then walked away. She closed her mouth with a snap. Now, what was Emma going to say to her, letting another security team sweep in and rescue her?

She shoved herself up against the headboard, awkwardly tucking pillows behind her. She stared at the window, trying to make sense of what had happened. A tap at the door drew her eyes that way, and she watched as the door cracked open once more and someone peeked in.

"Oh good, you're away. Stephen said you were, but I wasn't sure if you were still up or not. I'm Naomi." She stood at the side of the bed. "Now, tell me what we can do for you."

Candace held up her hand. "Lose this for one thing."

Naomi laughed.   "Stephen will be right back to pull it. You've had enough of that. We'll get you back on your feet again." She snuck a look at the door, then whispered in a conspiratorially manner.   "There's someone out there who really wants to see you.   We'll get you cleaned up, in some clothes and then we'll send him in or take you out to the living room. I'm sure you'd like a chance of scenery."

Candace shook her head. "Can't say that I wouldn't like that, seeing as I don't remember much about the last ten days or so, or however long it was."

"I get that, but you really do want to leave this room. Phoebe's been cooking and she's got some really good smelling broth and soup ready for you."

Chapter 12

$\mathcal{L}$ooking up against the bright sun, Jonah studied the sky, then looked back down at the field. He could see Leslie working away on the other side and smiled. Leslie had certainly stepped in and made a difference in his day. He paused, coming to a decision, and headed for his home office. He stopped as he saw the car sitting there, a car he didn't recognize. Pulling out his phone, he sent a text message to Leslie, asking him to come to the house.

He approached the car with caution, waiting back from it as the driver's door open and a man stepped out. He frowned, feeling like he should know the man.

"Jonah? It's been a lot of years." The man waited for Jonah's response.

Jonah remained silent, hearing steps coming behind him. Leslie stopped beside him, eyes watchful.

"A bodyguard isn't necessary, Jonah." The man waited for Leslie to leave. When he didn't, he shook his head. "Okay, so that's how you want to play it. I'm an old friend of your father's. Just stopped in to say hi to him."

"Not his property. Now, I would ask that you leave."

"That's not very friendly, Jonah. I'm here to help you."

"I don't know you. So I suggest you leave. There is a patrol car on its way."

The man stared at him for a moment, then pulled a business card from his pocket, holding it out to Jonah. Jonah didn't move and the man dropped the card to the ground. "Talk to your father and then call me."

The two younger men watched as the car pulled away. Then, Leslie had his phone out, sending in the plate number. He turned and stared as Jonah as Jonah picked up the card by its edges.

"Do you know who that was?" Leslie's voice held a hint of steel.

"It says Dominic Brown on the card. I don't remember ever hearing that name."

"The car is registered to a numbered company. I've asked that one of the detectives look a little harder at it."

Jonah nodded. "Why don't we ask Samuel's father to look into it as well?"

Leslie nodded, his phone out once more. Then, turning in a circle, he finally spoke.

"Someone's out there, Jonah."

"I know. Listen. I want to talk with you. How be we have an early lunch and talk?"

Leslie watched him for a moment, then nodded. "If you're offering me a job, permanent like, I'll take it. I went into police work because I needed to do something. This, here on the farm, is what I love."

Jonah stared to laugh. "That's exactly what I was going to do. We make a good team, Leslie. You have a touch that I haven't seen in a long time, with the plants and crops. My grandfather was like that."

"Thanks, Jonah. Maybe I can swing it to work only part-time with the department. Anyway, thanks."

"Not a problem, Leslie. You've what, twenty years in now?"

"I do. I joined when I was 18. I was holding off on retiring until later, but you know what? The time's right. Besides you need someone around here with you. You're still not safe."

"No, I don't think I am." Jonah's mind turned to what needed to be done and that set the tone for the conversation over the next hour or so. Jonah finally stretched.

"I'm heading into town with the orders. See you later or maybe just in the morning."

"Go see your lady, Jonah. I'll lock up." Leslie grinned as he strode away.

❦ ❦ ❦ ❦

Jonah stood on Andrew's porch late that afternoon. He stared around, feeling eyes on him. Now, why would that be? He still wasn't convinced he was in danger, but knew Candace certainly was. He turned as Silver opened the door.

"Jonah. How nice of you to come visit me!"

144

Jonah stared at her, then began to laugh. "Just who I wanted to see, Silver. How are you today?"

She laughed as she closed the door behind him. "I'm doing well. Candace is sitting out on the back deck. Go on through. Can I get you anything?"

"No, thank you. I'm good. I'll just grab a coffee on the way through. Does Candace need anything?"

"Not at the moment. Phoebe called and said both she and Andrew wouldn't be home until later but she left supper in the fridge." She tilted her head. "Somehow I think you're staying."

He grinned. "I just might be. Thank you, Silver, for what you've been doing."

She nodded as she watched him walk through to the back door. Then she shook her head. Whatever was going on, Candace had certainly found herself a gentleman. She sighed, wondering if that would ever happen for her.

Candace looked up as she saw boots stop in front of her. Her eyes lit up as she saw Jonah standing there.

Jonah studied her for a moment, then joined her on the bench.

"How are you feeling today?"

She shrugged. "I'm not sure. I'm stronger but there's something I just don't get. Why me, Jonah? What are they after?"

Jonah shrugged. "I think it has something to do with what you're doing, what you're providing. I've been asked to help search out fraudulent organic growers. Though how I do that, I'm not quite sure." He stopped speaking, his eyes staring into the distance, jumping a little as he felt a hand on his. He turned, catching the look in Candace's eyes.

"Jonah! What has happened since I've been gone? Andrew wants to talk to us tonight about what's going on. But, what's happened to you?" She studied his face. "No, don't hide it from me. I need to get this over with."

Jonah nodded. "I do too. That way we can start dating." He smiled as her mouth opened and then closed without her saying anything. "Yes, I'm serving you notice right here and now. I want to date you, Candace."

She nodded, her eyes leaving his face and tracking through the yard. "Will it ever be over, Jonah?"

"I pray it is soon, and that neither one of us is hurt again. When you were missing, Candace, I felt like part of me was gone."

She nodded, then looked around as she heard the door open. "There's Andrew. Somehow, I don't like the look on his face."

"I don't think I will either." Jonah stood as Andrew approached. "Afternoon, Andrew."

"Jonah. Candace." Andrew sank into one of the chairs, a sigh of relief coming from him. "It's nice to sit for a while. It's been one of those days." He took a look at Candace. "I heard from your cousin again. She really tries to look after you, doesn't she?"

Candace nodded, a frown on her face. "She does and she needs to stop. Next thing I know, all of Abe's guys and their ladies will be here."

Jonah stared at her. "And that would be bad?"

She nodded. "It would." She sighed. "I know they love me but having eight men and their ladies around kind of stretches what I can handle."

"Eight, huh?" Jonah shared a look with Andrew. "Why would it be that bad?"

"Because it just would." She stared at Andrew. "Now, what is it you wanted to talk to us about?"

"Nothing like be direct, Candace." Jonah shook his head. "Andrew just got home."

"I know he did, but I want to go back to my home. It's time."

Andrew shook his head. "Not a good idea, Candace."

She stood and stared him down. "It's my life, Andrew, and my home. I need to do this." She walked away from them and into the house.

Jonah watched, then spoke. "That went well, Andrew. Want to try again?"

Andrew shook his head. "No, I don't. I wanted to talk to you first anyway."

"About what?" Jonah turned his attention to his friend.

"That plate number? We've traced the company. It's part of the cartel that we've been looking at for a while now. You know, the one that has the fraudulent organics going."

"So, why come to me?"

"More than likely to see how much you know about it. I talked to your father. He doesn't know the man."

"Then our instincts were right this morning. How many more will they send?"

Andrew shrugged. "Enough to keep you busy about that and your mind off Candace." He paused, not quite sure how to proceed. "About Candace. I've done some checking on her." He held up his hand. "Don't say anything. It's standard for us to do that, and you know that already without me having to say anything. She's clean, just like I expected her to be." He stared at the door, as if waiting for Candace to come back. "The guard Richard brought in for us hasn't been too helpful. He's low in the chain of command, never saw the boss, and doesn't know what's going on. We've moved him from here to an undisclosed location for now."

"So, where do we sit then, Andrew? Did you ever get an identity on the body?"

"We did, but we're not releasing the name or any information on him. The knife was from Candace's work kitchen, and has been wiped clean under the blood spatters. So, that doesn't help us either."

Jonah shook his head. "When will it end, Andrew?"

"Hopefully soon. Listen, I hear you've gained a permanent worker."

Jonah grinned. "I did. Leslie's been working out great. He says he's ready to retire."

"I know he is. He has been for a while now." Andrew sighed. "He's one of the best we have."

Jonah grinned. "He loves working out there in the fields. I almost have to drag him out of them."

Andrew nodded, a thoughtful look on his face. "Any more letters or strange calls?"

Jonah frowned. "How'd you know?" Andrew grinned, and Jonah groaned. "That was a shot in the dark, wasn't it?"

Andrew nodded. "Just make sure I get them all, okay? Now, let's eat. I'm sure you're wanting to get home soon, right?" He laughed at the look on Jonah's face. "Come on, my friend. Let's go find our ladies."

Candace stood in the living room, her eyes on Jonah as he came back in, before she turned and walked quickly to her bedroom. She sat, feet bouncing. She needed to go home but it didn't look as if that would happen. She looked up as a tap came to her door.

Phoebe stood for a moment, watching her house guest, before she spoke. "We're getting ready to eat, Candace."

Candace shook her head. "I'm fine, Phoebe. Not really hungry tonight."

"Are you sure? Jonah was wanting to spend some time with you."

Candace sighed. "To tell you the truth, Phoebe, I want and need to go to my own place. You have been more than gracious, but this isn't home."

Phoebe nodded. "Then, we'll take you home. Gather your belongings, Candace. I'll take you."

Candace started to shake her head. "You can't do that. Andrew won't let you."

"He'll support me, Candace. You need to do this. It's Jonah that will have issues with it."

Candace gave a small smile. "He'll just have to accept it." She stood, looking around. "I don't think I have much, other than what I'm wearing that belongs to you."

Phoebe agreed, then reached for her purse and keys. "Let's go then. Andrew will figure it out."

Andrew stood and watched as the two women headed out the door, then turned to Jonah. "I think our ladies just walked out on us."

Jonah froze, then brushed by Andrew to watch from a window at the front. "And now where would they be going?"

"I suspect Candace has asked to go home. She needs time, Jonah, to absorb all

that's happened to her. Call her tomorrow.
Send her flowers. Show up with chocolates
or fruit or whatever it is she likes."

Jonah nodded. "In other words, court
her."

Andrew smiled. "That's exactly what
I mean. I didn't get a chance to do that with
Phoebe and I'll always regret it. But we've
turned our life into one long courtship."

Chapter 13

Candace turned in circles in her business kitchen the following Monday. She was back at work, but didn't feel like she should be. Ev sat on a nearby stool and watched.

"Talk to me, love. Tell me what you're thinking."

"What I'm thinking? That there was a body in that freezer over there." She pointed to it. "All my stuff I worked to obtain and purchase, my supplies, had to be tossed. Now, I feel like I'm starting over."

Eve nodded. "You are in a sense. But this time, you're not on your own. I'm serious about hiring on with you as a cook. I'm bored with the diner. And my staff don't need me looking over their shoulders all the time."

Candace studied her friend. "You're not just saying that, are you?" When Ev shook her head, Candace nodded hers. "Well, then, I guess I have a cook. It's not something I particularly have enjoyed."

Ev stood to hug her, then sat back down, pulling a pad of paper and pen towards her. "Let's make our plans, then, love. Where do we start? Your clientele is growing. I'll cook, you plan and visit. How does that sound?"

"It sounds about right." She paused for a moment as she heard the front door and then footsteps, a lot of footsteps. She didn't turn, her eyes squeezing shut in dismay.

Ev was trying to contain her laugher at the look on Candace's face.

"Aren't you ever going to turn around, Candace?"

She shook her head. "I know what I'm going to see, so let's pretend I did and they left?" She ended her statement in a question.

Laughter broke out behind her and she finally turned. Abe's men stood there, shoulder to shoulder watching her, their ladies standing in front of them.

"Now that makes a very formidable wall there, Candace." Ev finally gave into her laughter. "Care to introduce me?"

Candace stared at the men, her eyes going face to face until she reached Emma and Abe. "You just had to, didn't you, Emma?"

Emma laughed as she came forward to hug her cousin. "They wanted to see you, Candace, and you wouldn't come our way."

Candace shook her head as she made her way to each one, greeting them. They finally just milled around her kitchen and reception area. She heard the door at the back open and someone enter. She soon found hands on her shoulders and the eight men stood facing her once more.

"Good afternoon, Candace. Have some company, I see." Jonah's voice came from behind her.

She leaned back on him. "I do. You've met Abe, Emma, Ian and Murphy. This is the rest of his crew and their ladies." She quickly made introductions, missing the speculative glances thrown at Jonah.

Jonah met the glances without flinching, knowing he was being assessed. He finally spoke.

"Listen, your kitchen's not big enough for all of us. Why don't we adjourn to the farm? Can you leave?"

She shook her head. "Not for a couple of hours. Ev and I have some meals to get ready."

Ev shook her head. "Off with you, Candace. We've planned what we want for today and I can handle it. Go. Spend some time with your friends."

Candace turned to stare at her before nodding. "I guess we're planning a party then, Jonah."

Jonah wandered his fields with Abe and his men, questions thrown at him by all of them. He could tell they were serious in their work and assessments but knew how to relax and have fun. He didn't think he had enjoyed an afternoon quite as much in a long time. His group of friends was changing with some marrying and that put a different dynamic to them.

Candace had spent her afternoon just having fun with the ladies and her cousin. It had been a long time since she had relaxed so much. The men could hear the ladies' laughter and gentle teasing wafting across the breeze to them.

Late that afternoon, Jonah followed Candace to her home, getting out to stare around. He finally shrugged. How would he know what or who to look for? He put on a good show, but it really didn't make that much difference. He had talked to Andrew earlier and learned that the guard they had in custody had finally remembered some names and phone numbers. Bill and Lily were hard at work, but Andrew didn't think it would make much difference, yet. They were after the top guy and hadn't found the one trail to him.

Candace turned at the door, her eyes searching Jonah.

"You're quiet, Jonah."

He nodded. "Just a lot on my mind. I spoke with Andrew. The guard is coming up with names and numbers for them."

"That's good, isn't it?"

"It is if it leads them to the leader soon. If not, we'll still need to take precautions. I don't like it that you're having to go around on your own."

"Jonah." She waited until he looked at her. "We've had this out already. I have to live my life. I can't hide. Neither can you."

He sighed, his eyes searching the sky for the words he wanted to say. "I know, but I don't want to lose you, Candace. You've become very important to me, even though we haven't known each other for long."

She waited for him to continue. "What exactly are you saying, Jonah?"

"I'm saying I would like to take you out for dinner, bring you flowers, take you for walks, learn to know you better. In short, in old fashioned terms, I want to court you, Candace." He looked at her, uncertainty in his voice and face. "I'm so afraid something will happen to you."

She stood, her eyes on him, not quite comprehending what he was saying. She finally nodded. "I would like that, Jonah, but it's so dangerous right now. Abe's men threatened to take me back with them, or at have some of them move here until it was all over."

"I know. They all talked to me. But I think Richard or even Don should be sufficient if we need someone. If not, then I'll whisk you away to them."

"You would do that? Jonah, you have your farm to work."

"I know, just like you have your business. But God has brought in two people for us, Leslie for the farm, Ev for you."

She finally nodded. "You need to get home, Jonah. You have stuff to do you didn't get done today."

He stood for a moment, then leaned over to drop a kiss on her cheek. "Good night, sweetheart. Call me if you need to."

Hand on her cheek, Candace watched him walk away, before she turned to enter her house, her thoughts on what he had said instead of what she was going through.

❦ ❦ ❦ ❦

The man stood in the shadows of the building watching as Candace and Ev moved around inside, their laughter spilling out to him. He grimaced. He wanted this over but he had to wait. He hadn't been given permission yet to end it all. He turned, searching the area. He was alone but he felt eyes watching him. He couldn't see anyone but couldn't shake that feeling.

Silver brought her phone up, searching for the camera app and snapping a photo, sending it on to Richard before she called him.

"Candace has a watcher. He's outside her shop. I just sent you his picture."

"Good work, Silver. What are you doing there anyway?"

"Just stopping in to visit a friend. Do I need to move in on him?"

"No, watch him. I'll make the call."

Silver watched as the man stood restlessly, head constantly turning. She heard the sounds of tires and looked around to the front where an unmarked cruiser had pulled in. The man looked as well and then turned to walk away, stopping abruptly in his tracks as he saw the uniformed officer standing there. Handcuffed, he was shoved into the cruiser.

Silver debated about going in to see Candace and decided it was not likely a good move. If she heard about the arrest and Silver showed up, then she would figure out that Silver had been behind the arrest. Not what Richard wanted happening.

Candace turned her head as she heard a car pull into the parking lot and then leave. She shrugged, her mind more on the lists she was making than what was going on outside. Ev watched for a moment, before heading to the back door and stepping outside. She couldn't see anyone but she certainly had the feeling someone had been there.

Lord, when will it end, she thought. These two young people need to get on with their lives. I can see Candace opening up to You in a way I haven't seen in years.

She hesitated before going back in, taking time to walk around the building. She knew Candace would wonder where she had gone and why, but she needed to do this. Candace's mother wasn't there, but she was. She would take care of her as best she can.

"Ev, do you have the list of the new clients you talked to yesterday?" Candace's

162

voice met her as she entered the building once again.

"I do. I put it on the desk, right here. At least, it was here. I set it there before I left. Now, what happened to it?" Ev and Candace searched but couldn't find it. "That's strange, Candace. No one was here when I left. But I do remember their names. Let's make that list again." Eve reached for pen and paper, making a mental note to call Andrew. Someone had been in the building after all, getting past the security system.

Jonah turned as Leslie approached him later that morning.

"Jonah, I'm ready to head out with that delivery for you."

Jonah nodded, his eyes watching the road. Something was out there, or someone, but he couldn't see them.

"Did you notice anything odd this morning when you drove in?"

Leslie shook his head. "No, I didn't, but I feel someone out there, Jonah. I'm not sure it's a good idea to leave you on your own."   His hand reached down to rub Rusty's head. "Do you see anything?"

Jonah's head shook. "No, but I feel someone." He sighed. "I want this over. Like in yesterday."

Leslie grinned. "That was quite the crew that was here the other day."

"Abe's?   They are.   Candace was ticked at her cousin for bringing them all over."

"But I notice she had a good time with the ladies." Leslie paused, not quite sure how to continue. The eight men had all found their way to him at some point during the afternoon, quickly realizing he had been in law enforcement. "The men all talked to me about security and how to keep you two safe."

"I'm sure they had a lot of suggestions."   Jonah turned in a circle, trying to decide where he was being watched from.

"Actually, no.   They know what Andrew has suggested and that you're not doing." He grinned again at the look on

Jonah's face. "So, they decided they'd just drop by every few days if they're not away."

Jonah groaned. "Please, not that. Candace won't be happy at all. She told me she feels smothered sometimes where they're around."

"I can see that. They do have a tendency to that, but that's what makes them good at what they do. Abe's group is the best I've ever seen. Don and Richard are right up there as well."

"That's comforting, but I don't think it will help with Candace." He sighed, finally looking at Leslie. "What aren't you telling me?"

Leslie shrugged. "Just an idea I have. I've been in law enforcement for a long time, Jonah. I have heard things on the street, things that were just rumours or shadows. This is one of them, this about your farm. Someone is trying to take you down and destroy what your family has built up for years." He paused, not quite sure how to continue. "I don't think this has to do with Candace. Someone has been watching you, saw your interaction that first day at the market, and then targeted her to get to you. They're playing you both, trying to get one of you to break first."

Jonah stared at him. "What does Andrew say?"

Leslie shrugged. "He's not saying, nor is Bill. But I can guarantee you they've been thinking along those lines as well."

Jonah ran his hands through his hair and then groaned, looking down at the dirt on his hands. "Why'd I just do that? Back to what you were saying. Do you have any idea or suspicion as to why?"

Leslie just shook his head. He had a good idea and wanted to talk to Andrew first. Jonah's question would have to wait until another day.

"I'll head in with the deliveries. I think the field farthest from the house is about done now."

"I agree. We'll need to pull the vines from there over the next week. Not a job I enjoy."

Leslie laughed at the look on Jonah's face. "This year, buddy, you have help."

Chapter 14

 Jonah hesitated for a moment as he walked towards Candace's home that Sunday morning. He had talked her into driving to church with him and then going somewhere for a meal. He looked down at the flowers in his hand. He hoped she liked them. After he picked them, he realized he didn't know what flowers she liked. He sighed. It was going to be a long day, he thought.

Candace stood just inside the door, watching as Jonah stopped, then walked towards her, her face lit with a smile. She could almost hear the talk he was giving himself.

"Good morning, Jonah."

Jonah looked up, his steps hesitating again. "Good morning, Candace. You're beautiful this morning." The words blurted out before he caught them and then he groaned to himself.

Her face lit up even more. "Thank you, Jonah." She waited as he stood in front of her. "Are those for me?"

"What? Oh, these? They are. I'm sorry. I didn't know what flowers are your favourite."

She gave a small laugh, reaching to take the bouquet of daisies from him. "Whatever ones you plan to give me will be my favourite."

He grinned, waited for her to put the flowers into water, and then reaching for her hand, tucked her into his truck. He watched carefully to see if they were being followed or watched, and then sighed. How would he know anyway? He was certain someone was out there.

Candace watched as well, but her attention was mainly on the man sitting beside her, his hands loose on the steering wheel. She sighed to herself. He's a good man, Lord, just not sure if I should go out with him or not. I don't want him hurt.

Andrew watched them from where he was standing at the back of the church, Phoebe sitting beside them. He was worried. They hadn't gotten anything from the man they had picked up the other day and he knew they couldn't keep him in custody long. Now what, Lord, he asked. We need to get this over with and it's not happening.

Silas watched from the front of the church as the service concluded. He knew there were undercurrents swirling around but he wasn't sure who or what was needed to resolve them. His eyes caught the look on Andrew's face as he kept his attention on Jonah and Candace. Being the pastor that he was, Silas knew he'd be talking to the two of them this week to see how they were doing. His heart echoed the prayers of the group of friends. Let this be over soon, Lord.

❦ ❦ ❦ ❦

Jonah shifted the crates he was carrying in order to open the door at the diner, reaching to set them on the counter just inside the door. He waved at the staff and then walked back out the door, hesitating as he saw someone standing by

169

his truck. He looked around, not quite sure what was happening.

The man straightened as Jonah approached, his eyes flickering around the area.

"Can I help you?" Jonah stopped walking before he reached the man.

"Yeah, you can. You hiring?"

Jonah shook his head. "Sorry, I'm not and I don't know of anyone who is."

The man nodded, gave a word of thanks and then walked past Jonah, his hand dipping into Jonah's jacket pocket and out quickly. Jonah stood watching him walk away and then slid behind the wheel of the truck. He drove away, finally stopping in an almost empty parking lot to pull out the slip of paper he had been given.

Now what, he thought, as he read it. He looked around and then pulled out, heading for the police department. Once inside, he was led to Andrew's office, where he stood in the doorway, waiting for Andrew to lift his head.

Andrew looked up, a frown in place as he saw Jonah. Then he pointed at a chair and sat back in his own.

"What brings you by, Jonah? I wasn't expecting to see you today." Andrew watched as Jonah reached into his pocket and then stared at the paper in his hand.

"When I came out of Ev's diner, a man was waiting. Scruffy but tidy, if you get what I mean. He wanted to know if I was hiring. When I said no, he passed me and dropped this into my pocket." Jonah stared at the paper again before passing it onto Andrew.

Andrew searched Jonah's face as he reached for the paper. Reading it, he frowned.

"Did you know the man at all?"

Jonah shook his head, then realized Andrew wasn't watching him. "No. I think I've seen him around town, but he's not someone I know."

Andrew nodded, not telling Jonah that the man was an undercover officer and the one responsible for getting Candace free.

"This is curious, though." He read through the note again. "He's warning you."

"That's what I thought, too. But why? How would he know what's going on?"

Andrew barked out a small laugh. "Jonah, do you think most people in town haven't heard what's been going on with you and Candace? They're all working to help find out who the culprits are, and you should know that. You've from this town."

Jonah sat back, his eyes thoughtful. "Yeah, I guess they would, wouldn't they? So what about the note?"

"We'll look into it, but you and Candace need to be extra careful from now on. They mean to take one of you again, from what this note says, and use you against the other. I would suspect they'll look at taking Candace, given the investigation into the organics fraud we working through."

Jonah stared at him for a moment, not quite sure how to respond. "I just don't get it, Andrew. What is the big deal?"

"Fraud. They can charge more for organic products than the usual. And they make money if they use regular products as organics."

"Yeah, but they have to have certification that they're an organic farm." Jonah's voice died away as he caught the implication and his head dropped back as he groaned. "That's what it's all about, isn't it? Take me out of business and they can have a monopoly of fake organics. But they have to have the produce tested every so often."

"And they bring in organic products to do that. Have you noticed any missing from your place?"

Jonah's eyes shot to Andrew's as he realized what he was saying. "You're saying they're using mine to do this?" At Andrew's nod, he continued. "But if they take me out of the picture, then whose do they use? They go on to the next organics farmer, don't they, and the cycle continues for who knows how long." He rose and started pacing. "Andrew, we need to stop this."

"And we will. We've picked up a few more of the men involved, all small fry, but we're working our way up. That's no consolation to you or Candace. Who knows how long this will take, and you two have had to put your lives on hold while this is going on.”

Andrew leant his arms on his desk as he watched Jonah pace, his mind racing as to how they could end it quickly. He could come up no good plan to do that. Anything they tried would put both his friends at risk, and he wanted to avoid that at all costs. Lord, I could use a plan about now. I’m at a loss as to what to do. And I know Bill is too. What do we do, Lord?

Jonah suddenly spun, his eyes hard, his face determined. “I know exactly what I’m going to do, Andrew.”

“Now, wait a minute, Jonah. You need someone to work with you, whatever it is you’re planning.”

Jonah headed for the door. “I have someone, as many someones as I need.”

Andrew stared after him, trying to determine just how serious he was and what he would be up to. Then, shaking his head, he bent back over his paperwork, finally throwing his pen down and rising, heading to find Bill or Lily. Neither were in the building, and he hesitated, finally reaching for his keys and letting dispatch know he was out of the office. He needed to talk to someone and that someone was a two hour drive away.

Chapter 15

*C*andace moved around her backyard, restless in spite of the fatigue that weighed her down. She had not slept well now in days, and she knew why. She was constantly watching for whoever it was that was after her. She also worried about Jonah. She hadn't seen him in a couple of days and was concerned. She turned as she heard a car door close and the faint sound of her doorbell ringing. She headed back inside, standing to the side of the front door as she peeked out a window. She didn't know the man standing there, at least she didn't think so. She watched as he rang the doorbell again and then moved back to the sidewalk, his eyes searching the area and then staring at her door, almost as if he could see her. She moved silently away, reaching for her phone in her purse, then back to window to quickly snap his photo. She sent it on to Andrew, hoping to have an answer.

The man walked back to his car and stood, arms leaning on the roof, as he waited. She watched as Jonah pulled in beside him, then stood talking to him. It was almost as if Jonah knew he would be there.

Her phone chimed with a message from Andrew, assuring her that he knew the man and wanted her to speak with him. She shook her head. Who was this man and why was he here?

Jonah tapped at her door and waited while she opened it. He stepped through, his eyes on her face, before pulling her into a hug.

"Are you okay, Candace?"

She shrugged. "I have no idea. Who is that out there? I don't hear from you for a couple of days and then you show up here with him."

Jonah just tightened his arms around her, his chin on her head. "He's a good friend, not from around here. He's come to work on the farm with Leslie and I part time and I would really like it if he could do your deliveries for you."

She pushed back from him, anger on her face. "And why would I want to do that?"

Jonah ran his hands through his hair. He hadn't handled this right.

"Can we talk, Candace, without shouting, please? My friend out there, Sean, is a private investigator, but he deals with protection as well. That isn't known about him. He lives a good three hours from here. He's been investigating organics fraud for a while now, and wanted in on this. No one would know that, other than we've hired him to work part time for each of us. I hate the thought of you out there doing your deliveries on your own. It's a perfect way for them to get ahold of you again."

Candace stared at him, then walked away to the kitchen, leaving him standing there, hands shoved into his jeans' pockets. She peeked back around the door.

"You might as well ask him to come in then, seeing as you've made all these arrangements. I'm not saying yet that I'm going along with them." She disappeared and he heard the water running into the coffee carafe.

He opened the door and beckoned for his friend to come in. Sean shot him a quick look, and Jonah shrugged.

"Is she okay with this?" Sean kept his voice low, his eyes searching Jonah's face.

Jonah shrugged. "I didn't handle it very well, Sean. I think we may need to talk her into it."

Sean nodded. "Not a problem. Listen, I can come back if you like."

"No, you're here now. Come on. Let's go get some coffee and hopefully it's drinkable."

"What?" Sean stopped him with a hand on his arm.

Jonah gave a low laugh. "I was talking to some friends of hers the other day. She was ticked off enough at them once that when she made coffee, they couldn't drink it, she had made it that strong."

Sean laughed. "Then we'll have to hope she's not that ticked off with you today."

Jonah shook his head and cautiously peeked over at Candace. He couldn't read the look on her face. He sighed to himself.

In his rush to protect her, he forgot an important part of being a couple. He should have talked to her first.

"Candace, I'm sorry."

She cut him off before he could continue, her eyes on Sean. "Jonah, don't. I know why you did it. I just wish we had discussed this first. I'm Candace by the way." She held out her hand to Sean.

"And I'm Sean O'Dell. Nice to meet you."

"Sit. And yes, Jonah, the coffee is drinkable. I know what Micah told you the other day."

Jonah stared at her, his mouth open. "How'd you do that?"

"I know Micah. He's never let me forgot that." She sat, a glass of water in her hands. "Now, what was that plan you didn't discuss with me?"

Sean choked on his mouthful of coffee. Jonah shook his head even as a smile crossed his face.

"Sean works for me in the morning and for you in the afternoon, doing your deliveries. Leslie's on board with this. I had to ask him seeing as it affected his work hours."

She nodded, her eyes on Jonah. "And how do we explain this?"

Jonah shrugged. "Guess I haven't thought that out yet."

Sean watched the two interact before he spoke up. "Okay, you two. Enough. Work it out between yourselves later. Right now, we need to work this through to keep you both safe. Candace, if I may?"

They both looked at him, Jonah with interest, Candace with a closed look on her face. She's hard to read, Sean thought.

"Okay, Candace. This is how we play it. I'm working with Jonah to learn the organics business from the ground up. With you, I'm working to see how you use organics in your business and in doing that, I make your deliveries to talk to your clientele about how they like your food and if they're happy with you using organic produce, etc, in your meals."

Candace stared at him, then rose to reach into her fridge. She pulled out two tomatoes, grabbed a plate and knife and set them in front of him.

"Go ahead. Slice both of these and taste them. Then you tell me which is an organic one and which one isn't."

Sean stared at her for a moment, took a look at Jonah, then sliced the tomatoes. He hesitated, not quite sure what she was going after, but he finally pointed to the one on the right.

"This is the non-organic one."

She sat back, not answering, her eyes steady on his. "Why do you say that?"

He shrugged. "It takes like a tomato grown in a greenhouse. This one has a fresh sweet taste to it." He pointed to the other tomato.

"Jonah, you should hire this guy. He's got it figured out."

Jonah broke out into laughter, which got even stronger as he caught the look on Sean's face. "She had you going there for a moment, didn't she, my friend?"

Sean grinned. "That she did. Now about splitting time with each of you. We need to keep it very simple, what we tell people, and make sure we are all on the same page. Candace, I'll need you to go with me for the first week. And then I'll be on my own."

She nodded. "Just how long do you plan on being here?"

"As long as it takes. I doubt it will last much longer, though."

Jonah nodded. "I agree. I think Andrew's getting close, and I know these guys have to be getting worried."

❦ ❦ ❦ ❦

Sean stood in the business kitchen, watching carefully as Candace packed up the meals Ev had prepared and sorted them into order for delivery. She looked up at him and beckoned him over.

"I usually start furthest away and work my way back. There's the map I have drawn up." She sighed. "It's getting to the point, with all the business Eve is bringing in, that I'll need to hire another driver. I certainly never expected it to grow like this."

"That's good news for you, Candace. Let me put these into my car and then we'll get started. How many are there now?"

183

"I have twenty right now. By next week, it will be over thirty." She chewed at a finger, finally looking up at him. "I know what you're thinking. I'm stupid to try and do all this. But there is just such a need out there."

He shook his head. "Not stupid. Ev should have waited for you to plan ahead, that's all. But it would have taken off anyway, no matter who was involved. You'll need to work on that driver this week. Do you have anyone in mind?"

She shook her head. "I was going to talk to the pastor and see if he knew of anyone. Sometimes, retirees will volunteer for things like this, just to have something to do."

"Well, there you go then. That sounds like a plan."

She nodded and reached to set the alarm before closing the door. "We get these delivered and return with the bags. Then we're free for the night."

❦ ❦ ❦ ❦

The woman standing watching narrowed her eyes as she saw Candace leaving with Sean. This was a new player, she thought. She pulled out her phone and sent a text, asking what the leader wanted her to do. She quickly moved to her vehicle to follow them.

Sean watched the vehicle behind them in his rearview mirror. They were being followed but Candace didn't seem to see that. He wanted to keep her from noticing that they were. He memorized the plate number and then during a break while Candace was discussing meals with the elderly woman sent a text off to his office to have the plate ran for him.

"We're all done now, Sean." Candace leaned tiredly back on the seat. "This is a lot of work, you know."

"And?" He gave her a smile.

"And it's so worth it. Some of these seniors don't see anyone for days on end, other than us."

"That's sad, you know." He looked around as they got out at her business. "Have you had anyone hanging around here at all?"

She shook her head. "I'm sure there has been, but I haven't seen anyone. Why?"

He shrugged. "It just makes sense that they would be watching you. I'm sure they're watching Jonah as well. You two are going on with your lives, but this is not over, not by a long shot."

"I know." Candace sighed, her face wistful. "I wish it was. I hate this, you know?"

He nodded. "I know you do. Here, let me grab those for you. Where do you want them?"

"On the shelf in the walk-in cupboard is good. Thank you Sean. I guess I'll see you tomorrow."

"That you will. I'll wait until you lock up and follow you home."

"That's not necessary." She stared at him, sighed and then shrugged. "Okay, who decided it was necessary?"

He just laughed, followed her home and then took off for where he was staying. He sent a text off to Jonah and then walked towards the downtown area. He had someone he needed to find.

Chapter 16

*L*ooking across the fields stretching out in front of him, Jonah's eyes watched Leslie moving through one of them, pulling tomato vines. The field growing season was ending and he would soon be working in the greenhouses exclusively until spring. He reached for his phone, looking for a message that said it was all over and found nothing.

He turned and headed for his office. He had paperwork to do and had been putting it off. Maybe he needed to hire a part-time secretary, he thought, then shrugged. He didn't want to bring anyone else it.

He sighed as he set his bottle of water on the desk, then settled himself into his chair, sorting through the mail and then looking over the bills, reaching for his chequebook. Two hours later, he finally sat back, the sealed envelopes he had been working on set into a neat pile. His attention turned to the pile he had been ignoring, junk mail, requests for quotes and whatnot as he called it.   Most of this was quickly dealt with. Then, his hand paused as he saw the last envelope.   No address on it, just his name.   His eyes raised and narrowed, he pondered how it had gotten there.

He carefully opened it and extracted the folded letter. He blanched as he read it, then scooping it and the envelope up, he ran for his truck, not seeing Leslie around to tell him he was off.

Bill looked up from his coffee at Ev's diner and watched as Jonah headed his way. He frowned.   Jonah's demeanour was not what he was expecting.

Jonah slid into a chair across from Bill, nodding at the waitress who approached with the coffee cup. He waited until she left before looking at Bill.

"Somehow, Jonah, I don't think this is a social call."

Jonah shook his head, as he reached into his jacket pocket. "It's not. I found this today with my mail. I have gone over it for about a week, just collected it from the box and dropped it on my desk. I usually do my bills and information requests on one day."

Bill reached for the envelope, noting it had been crushed by Jonah's hand. "It's that bad?"

Jonah nodded. "It is. I pray I'm not too late."

Bill stopped, his eyes on Jonah's face. "Too late for what?"

Jonah nodded at the envelope and the letter Bill had removed. "Read that. Then I need to go find Candace."

Bill's eyes dropped to the letter and his face hardened. They, whoever they were, had threatened Candace once more.

"They warn about Candace again I see"

Jonah nodded, the words from the letter inscribed on his heart.

Take the fall, Jonah. Walk away from your farm. Or else your pretty little sweetheart will disappear for good.

Bill stared at the paper, then up at Jonah. "I know you. That's not happening."

"No, it's not. So what do we do, Bill? Are you any closer to finding these people?"

Bill nodded. "We are. We're almost to the top of the chain but that person has stayed well hidden.   I spoke with Sean." Jonah stared at him when he said that. "I know. He wasn't supposed to talk to us, but he did, on an informal basis. He's given us some more information that we hope will find the top person."

Jonah sat back, his fingers tapping on the tabletop. "I pray it does. We need this over with, Bill.   Candace isn't sleeping much and I must say, I'm not either."

"What would happen if we had to stick you two away somewhere?"

Jonah shrugged.   "I don't like that idea, Bill, but our businesses could float for a while with the help we have. My fields are about done for the fall."

"Okay, then. This is what I need you to do. Continue on as you have been. Stay as safe as you can. Candace needs you to spend time with her." He paused, thinking through what he needed Jonah and Candace to do. He sighed. "We may have to tuck you away somewhere.

Jonah was shaking his head. "That's not happening, Bill. I won't live my life in hiding. Nor will Candace."

"Then, what do we do? I can't put any officers with you, and any security team I know of isn't available."

Jonah nodded. "I know. Abe's already threatening to stick her away at his place, and she bluntly told him off." He grinned as he remembered the heated conversation between the two and how the other men had gotten involved in it.

"I take it she refused?"

"That she did. Abe wasn't pleased." Jonah finally rose. "Listen, I know you can't do much, with just this and not knowing who is all involved. We'll do our best, that's all I can promise."

Bill watched as Jonah walked away, waving through the passthrough window at the staff in the kitchen. He sighed, as he pocketed the letter, dropped a bill on the table for his coffee, and headed out to find Andrew. This is getting old, Lord. How many more friends are going to have this happen to them. Like, there's two more of our group. He stopped, a puzzled frown on his face. Now, where had that thought come from? Then he was running for his car. A new thought had crossed his mind and he needed to do some research.

❦ ❦ ❦ ❦

Candace worked around her kitchen, making a list of supplies and produce she needed to get and then tidied away what had been used. Ev was gone for the day, and she relished the time alone. She didn't get that a lot any more. She finally turned, heading for the door and her car. She needed to source out more produce and meats. She was headed out of town to do just that, for the meats anyway. She had spoken to a beef farmer earlier that week and wanted more information from him. Sean stood and watched her leave, before he sighed. She wasn't supposed to be doing this, he thought. How do we keep her safe if she just walks away from us?

Candace knew that Sean had been watching her drive away. Today, she just needed to get away from it all. She had a packed knapsack in her trunk. She planned on just disappearing for the weekend and staying away from everyone. She pulled to the side of the road and sent Jonah a quick text, letting him know she was away and would be in touch Sunday night. *He won't be happy, now will he, Lord? But I need to do this. I need some time with just You. I haven't had that in a long time.*

She finally pulled into a small bed and breakfast, hoping there was a room for her, two hours away from Elmton, in the opposite direction of where she had first been headed that afternoon. She was soon settled into a room decorated in yellows, with daisies dancing across the comforter on the dark wooden four poster bed. She sighed. *This would work well,* she thought. *Lots of hiking trails around.*

❧ ❧ ❧ ❧

Jonah stared at the message from Candace and fear shot through him. She was gone for the weekend. How could she just run for away like that? Leslie stood near him, assessing him.

"Bad news, Jonah?"

He nodded. "I think so. Candace is gone for the weekend, on her own, and she hasn't told me where."

"And told no-one else, I suspect. I've been expecting her to do just this." He

193

paused as Jonah spun to stare at him. "She's hurting, Jonah, from what I don't know. She's scared. She doesn't want to be around you in case you get hurt."

"I don't care about me. I just want to know she's safe."

"As safe as she can make herself. We can't track her. And I think that was her plan. You'll find she was already out of town when she sent that text."

Jonah nodded. "I think you're right." He raised his eyes to the horizon. "There's goes my plans for the weekend."

Leslie laughed. "You'll have to make new ones then. See you on Monday." He walked to his truck and waving drove away.

Jonah watched him leave, then headed for one of the greenhouses. He would work this weekend, he guessed, not wanting to just sit around. He sighed as he studied the plants. This was not what he wanted to do today. Instead of entering the greenhouse, he headed for his house. He needed some time with God and knew just where he could do that.

"Hey, Jonah? You here?" Monday morning found Leslie looking for Jonah. He turned, puzzled. Jonah's truck was here but there was no sign of him. He tapped at the door before trying it. Unlocked, and he didn't like that. He made a swift search through the house and then headed for the greenhouses and the outbuildings. An hour later he stood, hand on his head, eyes searching the fields. There was absolutely no sign of Jonah. He reached for his phone and called it in. When did Jonah disappear?

Sean's steps slowed as he approached Leslie, his mind whirling at the look on the man's face.

"He's gone?"

Leslie spun at he heard a voice behind him, then nodded. "There's no sign of him, unless he's out in the fields somewhere, and I would see him if that was the case."

Sean too searched the fields, walking closer to them. "Then, I gather he's been taken somewhere."

"Yeah, it looks that way. I left about four on Friday. He had gotten a message from Candace that she had left for the weekend and he seemed to be at loose ends."

Sean nodded as he watched the emergency vehicles pull in. "I watched her leave. She didn't say where she was off to, but she was running." He pointed at the house. "Any signs you saw in there that gave a clue?"

Leslie shook his head. "I didn't see much, other than that Jonah wasn't there." He paused. "But come to think of it, his supper plate was still on the table and I don't think he had eaten much of it."

Sean drew a deep breath. "Come on, then. Let's go find out what we can."

❧ ❧ ❧ ❧

Candace looked up that evening from the book she had been reading, hearing footsteps coming up her walk. She hoped it was Jonah. She hadn't heard from him that day and that puzzled her.

She stood in the doorway, watching as Bill and Lily walked towards her, then raising her eyes, catching sight of Richard heading towards her as well. This is not good, she thought, and no, Lord, I'm not running any more.

"Bill?   What are you three doing here?"

"Can we come in, Candace? We really need to talk to you." Bill's voice gave no hint of what he wanted.

She stood back, pointing towards the living room. "Can I get you anything?"

The three shook their heads as they watched her curl up in her favourite chair and then stare at them, one at a time.

"You're here for a reason. Spit it out."

Richard choked back a laugh as Bill sputtered. Lily just grinned.

"Bill? I'm waiting." Candace's face didn't give away much but Richard could tell she was worried.

"It's like this, Candace. Where were you over the weekend?" Bill watched her face closely.

"I took some me time and went away. I spent the weekend at a lovely bed and breakfast two hours south of here. Now, why?"

Bill shared a look with the other two before he spoke again. "Leslie arrived for

197

work this morning and found Jonah missing. It looks as if he disappeared Friday night."

"Disappeared? How?" Candace's feet hit the floor with a thud as she sat upright, her eyes focused on Bill.

"We didn't find much evidence, but it looks as Bill let whoever it was into his home. His supper was still on the table."

"Rusty?"

"Rusty? Oh, his dog. Now, that's a strange thing. We didn't find him."

"Oh, no!   Rusty never leaves the property and he's glued to Jonah's side when Jonah is home."

Bill nodded. "We're looking for him as well. Sean and Leslie are searching the woods around the farm, and we put a call into animal control."

She stared at him, then at the other two. "So where does that leave us?"

"We need to put you somewhere safe. That's why Richard's here."

She stared at Bill, then at Richard. "Really?   You're sticking me away somewhere? Abe threatened that. You get the same answer that I gave him. It's not happening."

"We need to do this, Candace. They'll come after you to make Jonah do what they want."

"And just what do they want him to do? Do you know that?"

Bill shook his head. "Not yet. We think they'll be in touch with you in the next couple of days."

Candace stood and paced, finally turning to them. "Give me a couple of days to think this over. Then I'll give you an answer."

Richard finally spoke. "You may not have a couple of days, Candace."

She shrugged. "That's my answer. Now, I would like you all to leave."

Knowing they had no choice, the three rose and walked away, leaving Candace staring after them. Once they were gone, she almost ran to her bedroom, throwing clothes and her Bible into a backpack and grabbing her phone. She stared at it for a moment, then turned it off, sticking it into a side pocket. She reached for her purse, grabbing her ID, debit card and cash. She stood for a moment, then grabbing out her phone again, sent a quick text message to Ev, and turned her phone off again. She hesitated, her eyes lifted up in prayer, before extinguishing the lights, setting the security system, and slipping out the back door. She wasn't waiting for Bill to stick her away somewhere. She had been through this before. She knew how to disappear.

❦ ❦ ❦ ❦

Andrew turned as he heard Bill call his name the next day and waited for him to catch up before they were seated in Andrew's office. Andrew had a pretty good idea of what Bill was going to say.

"She ran?"

Bill nodded. "It must have been right after we left. Richard hung around but didn't see her go, but he was watching the front not the back. Ev got a message from her about thirty minutes after she told us to leave."

"She told you to leave?"

Bill nodded, a small smile creasing his face. "She basically did. Now we have no idea where either one of them are."

Andrew nodded, then spoke. "I have talked to Candace's father. She knows how to look after herself. It's not the first time she's disappeared like this, he tells me."

"It's not? Then why didn't we know this."

"Because we had no need to. He's given me some information as to how to find her. I've given it to Lily, so talk to her." Andrew handed Bill a paper. "Try finding these people. They might know where she is."

Bill nodded as he stood, his eyes on the paper. Then he frowned. "I don't think they will, Andrew."

"What do you mean?" Andrew looked askance at Bill.

"Because some of these are fictional characters. I'm not sure who's pulling whose leg, but someone is."

Andrew sighed. "I had the feeling something wasn't quite right. Okay, then call Emma. See if she'll talk to you."

"Somehow, I don't think she will. That whole group is very protective of

Candace, and I still haven't figured out why."

A voice at the door had Bill spinning around. Ian from Abe's group stood there.

"If I could talk to you two for a moment, I might have some information for you. And yes, we are very protective of her."

For the next hour, Ian, Bill and Andrew spoke, with Ian finally standing.

"That's all I know, Andrew. I'm not sure if it will help. Emma won't be happy with me if she knows I'm here, but Abe said he'd talk to her."

Andrew nodded. "Thanks for your help today, Ian."

Bill stared at the notes he had taken, and then sighed. "My work just tripled, you know that."

Andrew laughed. "Concentrate on that. Your other cases are being handled except where they need your direct involvement. Jason and Lily are investigating something else."

Bill nodded, finally looking at Andrew, his eyes puzzled. "There's something you're not telling me, Andrew."

Andrew sat back, his eyes on Bill. "I wish I could tell you, Bill, but for now, I have to keep someone's trust in me and keep their secret. If nothing is resolved in three days with this, then I'll talk to you."

Bill nodded again, turning to the door. "Then, I get right on this. Maybe this will break the case wide open." He waved his notes in the air as he walked away.

Andrew watched him go, then sat back once more in his chair, sighing as he did so. He studied the work on his desk before picking up his pen. There are times, Lord, when I wonder why I took on this position, but You know why. The phone ringing broke his concentration three hours later as he answered to hear Phoebe's voice. He frowned at her words, then hanging up, reached for her keys. Candace had been in touch with Phoebe and needed Andrew to talk to Phoebe without being at the office.

❧ ❧ ❧ ❧

Candace watched from the shadows in Andrew's back yard as he and Phoebe wandered their yard, getting closer to where she was hiding.   She hated to involve Phoebe, but knew that was the only way she could get to Andrew.

Andrew sat on the stump he had keep in the back, under the spreading oak leaves. Phoebe headed back for the house, leaving Andrew to wonder where Candace was hiding.

"I know you're here, Candace. I hope you have good reason for running."

"I do, Andrew.   They can't use me against Jonah if they can't find me."

"And who says they can't find you?"

"Trust me, they'd never find me."

"Are you going to show yourself?"

He heard a sigh behind him, before she spoke again. "I don't think so. That way, you can honestly say you didn't see me, only that I spoke with you."

He nodded. "Okay. You called this meeting. What's up?"

"First, have you heard from Jonah?"

"No, we haven't. We were hoping you had."

"I turned my phone off. I'll only have it on once in a while. And I know that will be a problem. Doing this will force them to call someone else."

"Or it could get him killed. Did you think of that?"

There was silence for a moment, and he heard the trace of tears in her voice when she spoke. "Believe me, Andrew, I have considered every possibility. I haven't done this lightly."

"That was the message Abe sent over with Ian."

She groaned. "Abe's weighing in? He needs to stay out of it. He's putting Emma and their son at risk."

"He knows that, Candace, but that's what he does for a living, protect people."

"I know. I still don't like it. Secondly, I've left an envelope for Ev under the flower box at the front. It has cheques that she'll need for the next week to ten days." She paused, and Andrew wondered if she was even still behind him.

"Andrew, I know where Rusty is. Whoever took Jonah took Rusty too. I just don't know if Jonah's there too. I couldn't find out."

"Leave me the address. I'll have it checked out. What else?"

She was silent, her eyes on Andrew, wondering that he trusted her that much.

"Why do you believe me, Andrew?"

"Because you are exactly who you say you are, you keep your word. You try your best to live as God would have you live."

She nodded, forgetting that he couldn't see her. "I've talked to Silas. He has more information for you, if you need it. I told him to bring it to you in two days if I haven't been back in touch."

Andrew sighed. "We need you to come in and be safe, Candace."

"Not happening, Andrew. It's not that I don't trust you and your officers. This is just something I have to do. I've done it in the past and it worked fine."

"What do you mean, done it in the past?"

"You didn't find out that little tidbit, did you? It's hidden well, under another name. I had a friend who threatened me, just because she thought I stole her boyfriend. I couldn't stand the man, and was glad when they broke up. Unfortunately, he tried to convince her I was the problem. She finally found out the truth, but it was too late. I had had to hide for a month. And someday I'll give you all the details. If I have to leave Elmton to be safe, then I will but somehow I don't think that's necessary at this point." Her voice died away.

Andrew waited for her to continue but finally realized she was gone. He stood, his eyes searching the shrubbery behind him before he shook his head. She really hadn't helped him out other than giving him the address where Rusty was. It would be a miracle if Jonah was at the same spot.

He shook his head as he reached for the slip of paper she had set down behind him. He knew he had to trust her but it was hard.

Chapter 17

$\mathcal{J}$onah rolled over on the floor, groaning from the pain of sleeping on the hard cold cement. He blinked, not quite sure how long he had been there. Not again, he thought. I can't be a captive again, could it? He struggled to sit, willing the nausea to dissipate. He searched the room, finally seeing the bottles of water on the table. He staggered as he stood and stopped, waiting for his head to stop spinning.

He heard the door opening and ignored it as he reached for the water, watching the bottle spinning away from him as it was knocked from his reach. He swayed, not as steady on his feet as he would like to be. He didn't heard the words directed at him that turned to shouts. His mind was fading and he sank to the floor where he stood, not feeling the boots that kicked at him.

The man turned and stomped to the door, anger evident in every stride. He turned once more to look at Jonah who hadn't moved. What did those fools do to him, he wondered?

He stormed through the building, looking for the two men who had brought Jonah to him. Heads would roll, he thought, and it wouldn't be his because someone else screwed up. The leader had been specific and he in turn had been specific. This was not how they wanted Jonah, drugged and unconscious. He couldn't do his part if he was.

❦ ❦ ❦ ❦

Candace watched the building, knowing Jonah was inside. She had been counting heads, up to five. She ducked even lower as an expensive car approached and a woman exited it, looking around before she entered the building.

She reached for her phone, eyes searching the area to ensure she was on her own. She was. She looked down, her fingers flying over her phone. She shut it down again once she had sent the text, secreting it in a pocket of her jacket. She didn't want it obvious but she didn't want to lose it. She had to figure out a way to get to Jonah. Waiting for help might now be an option. She moved slowly through the weeds and small bushes in the overgrown parking lot, her eyes scanning the area. She had no weapon, but she didn't think she'd be able to use one even if she did. Abe's men had made sure she was well trained in martial arts, telling her she needed to be able to take someone down if needed. She was glad now they had emphasized her training, even if they regretted that she could take each one of them down in a matter of seconds.

She reached the edge of the building and crept on silent feet towards the back, looking around for a way in. She finally saw a broken window, just wide enough for her to get in. She jumped to catch the frame of the window and carefully pulled herself up enough to look it. An empty office area greeted her. She dropped down on the inside of the building, waiting and listening. Hearing nothing she crept towards the open, broken down door. How long had this place be empty, she wondered?

She stood near the door, listening again, before stepping cautiously forward and searching the dimness. Dust motes floated in what sunlight made it through the dirty windows. She turned her head towards the voices she could hear, and then crept away from them, checking out doors as she went along. She found one that was locked, frustrating her. This must be where Jonah was, she thought. Now what? She heard footsteps heading her way and she ran to hide, her breath catching in her throat. She heard the men's voices, then the door being unlocked. She couldn't look, she thought, they'd see me.

She listened to the men's cursing, the footsteps walking way, sounding heavier than they had been. She finally peeked out from her hiding place, seeing no one. She scurried for the locked door and found it open, no one in there. She hesitated, looking behind her and then entered the room. Jonah was gone, if he had been here. Now what? She saw the reflections of the red and blue lights and headed for the window, landing softly on her feet outside the building and then running for shelter.

Andrew stood in the room Jonah had been held in, searching for anything that would help find him. There was nothing. His team would scour the area.

Bill headed his way, a thoughtful look on his face.

"We found small footprints, Andrew. We think they belong to a woman. They're under a window, looking like a sneaker. Then, there are a multitude of footprints near the front of the building, with what looks like a woman's high heels."

Andrew nodded. "I suspect the leader is a woman. That would make sense, don't you think?"

Bill stared at him for a moment before he spoke. "A woman? That's what you've been thinking?"

Andrew nodded as he walked back towards the front of the building. "That's what we should be thinking, Bill. The planning, the men involved, the reasons, it could easily be a woman." He stopped staring into the office area. "They've been here for a while. Have the team search here."

"I will. Where will you be?"

"Talking to Phoebe. She had contact with Candace the day or so after she disappeared. She set up a meeting with me. I was to give her two days and then bring you in. It hasn't been two days but we need to talk." Andrew reached for his phone. "I have an address here I'm heading over to. She seemed to think Rusty might be there."

"And you're just telling me now?" Bill was frustrated.

"Hold that thought, Bill."   Andrew walked away as he spoke on his phone, turning to watch Bill watching him.   He walked back towards him as he pocketed his phone.   "They've found Rusty.   He was running loose around the farm. Leslie thinks someone dropped him off."

"Dropped him off? So he could easily have been at that address? But who would do that?"

"I think the same person who told us where Candace was when she disappeared." Andrew sighed, knowing this was far from over. "Call me if you find anything, Bill. I think I need to go talk to Silas."

"Do that, Andrew.   Has the prayer chain been activated?"

"It has. Phoebe was told by Faith that it's set up to work around the clock. There's a lot of power in our friends' prayers."

"There is, Andrew. They'll pray them home, somehow."

❧ ❧ ❧ ❧

Candace crouched down in the doorway of a building downtown, her head on her knees, backpack tucked behind her. She was tired, but couldn't take the chance on sleeping. She raised her head, her eyes searching.   She was supposed to meet someone here, someone who said they had news of where Jonah was staying. Her head went back down and she slept, not hearing the footsteps walking towards her. The man stood, looked around, and then gathered her up in his arms. She didn't stir. He walked back the way he had come, sliding the sleeping Candace into the passenger seat of his car.   He stood for a moment, looking around, knowing that his life would be forfeited if he was found helping her.

Candace finally stirred, her eyes blinking open. She sat up abruptly, staring

214

around the room. She wasn't where she had gone to sleep. She scrambled to her feet, sliding off the bed and looking for her backpack. It sat near the door. She reached for the knob, turning it and opening the door. She crept through, looking around, jumping when a voice spoke from behind her

"Good. You're awake. I was just coming to find you."

She spun, staring at the man standing there, then relaxing. "Sean! Where did you come from? And were you the one I was supposed to meet."

He pointed to the kitchen. "Come, have some breakfast. You've slept for twelve hours."

She stopped, horror on her face. "Twelve hours? Oh no!"

He shoved her down in a chair and set toast in front of her. "Start with that, then let me know what you want."

She stared at the toast, blinking back tears. "Sean? Where are we?"

"I found you sleeping at our meeting place last night and brought you here. You're a sound sleeper, did you know?" He grinned as she made a face at him. "Anyway, I know they've moved Jonah and that you were in the building at the time. And Rusty has been brought home."

"So now what, Sean?" She nibbled at the toast, not really hungry, but knowing she needed to eat.

"We try and find him. I have some ideas as to where they may be. I'm pretty confident I know who the leader is."

"You are? Have you talked to Andrew then?"

"Not yet. I need a little bit more evidence that I can turn over to him." He watched her slump in the chair. "Don't give up hope, Candace. We're getting there. Have faith that God knows where Jonah is."

"It should but it's so hard, Sean. I went through something years ago and didn't ever want to go through something again."

🍏 🍏 🍏 🍏

Jonah sat slumped in a chair, his wrists fastened to the chair arms. He still hadn't come completely around, but was awake enough to hear the men talking behind him.

He realized that there was no way he would make it out alive, if what they were saying was true. He wanted to meet the one in charge, to find out why this had happened. It had to be money, he thought, all about money.

His thoughts swirled in circles, each plan chasing the other before he decided there was not way he would be able to free himself and make it out. He had to depend on someone finding him and that he didn't think would happen. He hadn't seen where he had been taken, but he had heard faint words letting him know he was now outside of town. Just where, he wasn't sure.

Footsteps sounded behind him as he hung his head, trying to think of a way out. His head was jerked back and he stared at the man standing in front of him. He frowned, trying to focus properly.

The man watched for a moment, before raising his eyes to stare at the two men with him.

"What did you two do to him?"

"Just gave him the drug like you told us to. Nothing more." The shorter older man sounded defensive.

"Then you must have given him too much."

"No, just the amount you told us to. Maybe you gave us the wrong amount."

The first man glared at the two, then focused on Jonah. "We'll have to wait until he recovers. Waiting is not part of the plan. She's not going to be happy. Heads will roll for this, mark my words."

The two men stared at each other and then at him before turning and walking away. They walked out of the building, shared a look and kept on walking. Both had had enough. They reached their vehicle and drove away, heading out of town and not looking back.

The man in front of Jonah, Tom by name, grabbed Jonah's hair and pulled his head up so he could see his face. He dropped Jonah's head back down. Now what, he thought, as he paced from the room. The leader would be here shortly and she would not be pleased as what she found. He would pay for it, he knew. He didn't hear the door open behind him and he turned, to meet a fist to the face that knocked him to the floor.

Sean stood over the man, then reached for the handcuffs he had tucked into his pocket. Pulling Tom's arms behind him, he quickly locked the cuffs, then turned his attention to Jonah. Two swift strikes with the knife and Jonah was free. Sean assessed him, then driving a shoulder into Jonah's abdomen, lifted him to his shoulders and walked quickly out of the building and across the grass to where he had hidden his car.

Candace watched as Sean appeared and shoved Jonah into the backseat. He stopped her from moving back there.

"Sit tight in the front, Candace. We need to get out of here and I don't have time for you to get settled with Jonah in the back."

"Is he alive, Sean? At least tell me that."

"He is." He pulled out his phone. "Here. Call Andrew. Let him know there's a man handcuffed on the first floor. He'll want to talk to him."

Candace hung up from her conversation with Andrew. "He says there's a patrol car a couple of blocks away and he'll send them. He asked that we wait."

"Not happening. Now, let's get ourselves out of here. Duck down where you can't be seen, okay?"

Candace nodded, peeking between the seats at Jonah, a distressed look on her face as he moaned with the movement of the car.

"How far, Sean?"

He stared at her, realizing that she was not thinking straight and had forgotten where he had taken her the night before. "Not far from here, Candace. I've been staying just outside the city."

Candace watched as Sean dropped Jonah gently on the bed. Then she moved forward, her hand going to his face.

"Can you check him out for injuries, Sean? I'm going to see if I can find a basin for some warm water. Then I'll need your help to clean him up."

Sean stopped her with a hand on her arm. "Bring me the water, Candace. I'll do it." He stared her down before she nodded and moved away. Sean moved quickly to assess Jonah, then stood back to stare at him.

Just some bruising on the ribs, not bad, but he is unconscious. What did they do to him?

He turned as he heard a tap at the door. Candace stood there, a basin of warm water in her hands, towels over her shoulder.

"Here you go, Sean. I'll see if I can find us something to eat."

He nodded and stood for a moment watching her walk away. He wouldn't have recognized her if he passed her on the street, what with the black wig with the pink and purple highlights and the black contacts. He grinned suddenly. No one who knew her would have seen that it was her. He set the basin down and went to find her.

"Candace? Why don't you get cleaned up yourself. There's a shower there. I think we can ditch your disguise."

She turned, a grin playing around her lips. "What? You don't like the new me?"

He gave a low laugh. "It's fine, but we need you normal for Jonah."

She spluttered as he walked away, grinning. She nodded as she watched him disappear. She did need to change and headed for her backpack.

An hour later, she sat at Jonah's bedside, watching as his head moved restlessly, his eyes flickering open and closed. His hand has held firmly in hers.

"What did they do to him, Sean?"

Sean stood, his shoulder leaning against the door jamb. "I would suspect they've drugged him in some way. But with what, I have no idea." He turned to look towards the door. "We need someone to draw blood to tell us exactly what."

"And how do we do that without blowing our hiding spot?" Candace turned to face him, a thoughtful look on her face. "I know someone who could and would."

He nodded. "I know you do. Do you want to call him?"

She shook her head. "No, because if I do, they'll take me away from here and from Jonah."

"Call him, Candace. This is about to break wide open and you may need to be far away form here."

"I'm not leaving Jonah."

"You love him, don't you?" When she refused to answer, Sean blew out a breath. "Fine. Don't answer. But call whoever it is you need to."

She shook her head again. "I can't, Sean. It would put his job at risk and I can't do that."

"Then what do we do? We can't take him to the hospital. We might have to, though, if he doesn't soon come around."

Sean pulled his phone out and walked away. He sent a quick text message to Andrew, letting him know he had both Jonah and Candace safe.

❧ ❧ ❧ ❧

Andrew turned in the board room to find Bill or Lily. Not seeing either one, he approached Jason Long, another of his detectives.

"Jason. I need you to do something for me. I know who now has Jonah and Candace. Sean says Jonah's out of it and they think he's been drugged but with what they're not sure."

Jason stared at him for a moment, lost in thought, then spun, staring at the room.

223

"They found something in that building that didn't fit. Here, we go. It's a sedative. That's what they would have used."

Andrew nodded, then sent off a quick text to Sean. "Any side effects that you know of?"

"It just takes a while to come out of it and we don't know how much he was given."

Jason nodded over Andrew's shoulder. "There's Bill and he looks as if he has some good news for a change."

Chapter 18

$\mathcal{J}$onah groaned as he rolled to his side, his eyes cracking open. He rubbed his hand over the blankets covering him and felt the pillow under his head. Where was he? Lord, did You really get me out there?

Sean shot a glance towards the living room where Candace slept on the couch, her face buried under her arm. Then he moved quietly into the room, around the bed so he could face Jonah.

"Jonah?" He waited, then said the name again.

"Sean? Is that you, buddy? Where are I?"

"You're safe, friend. We got you out and have hidden you away for now."

Jonah pushed himself up, his arms shaking as he did so. Sean stuffed pillows behind his back.

"How you feeling?"

"Horrible. What did they do to me?"

"Sedated you. Trying to keep you quiet until they could get to Candace."

"Candace!" Jonah pushed himself away from the pillows and reached for the blankets to shove them away so he could rise. Sean's hand on his shoulder stopped him.

"She's safe, Jonah. She's asleep in another room right now."

Jonah squinted at him. "You're sure? Then where are we?"

"In the cabin I've been using. Don't worry. We weren't followed and no one can track this."

"How's Candace?"

"She's tired, but glad you're safe." Sean stared at him for a moment. "Do you want anything right now? Here's some water. I think maybe something light to eat at first."

Jonah nodded, his eyes sliding closed again, the water bottle rolling from his relaxed hand. He slept, but this time it was not a drugged sleep.

"Is he okay?" A quiet voice spoke from the doorway.

"He is. He's sleeping now." Sean turned to watch her. "Let me get you some breakfast. Then we'll have to make plans."

She nodded. "Did he say anything?"

"Other than asking if you were okay, no." He pointed towards the kitchen.

Candace slid onto one of the wooden kitchen chairs and stared around at the rustic wooden cabinets. "How'd you find this place, anyway?"

"It belongs to a maternal great uncle. Don't worry. No one knows about it." He turned to watch her. "You got some sleep."

"I did. I must have needed it." She stared at the window. "What now, Sean? We can't stay here for long."

"No, we can stay here for a while. I talked to Andrew earlier."

"And he wants us to turn ourselves in."

"No, actually, he doesn't. He also doesn't want to know where we are. He has suggested that we find Richard or Don, or in the worst case scenario head for Abe."

"I don't want to bring this to them any more. It's bad enough that you're involved."

"It's what I do, Candace. How much has Jonah told you about me?"

"Other than that you're a good friend and he'd trust you with his life."

Sean nodded, his eyes searching her face. "Then, please trust me as well. I won't let anyone hurt you again. That goes for Jonah too."

They turned as they heard shuffling in the hall and Jonah appeared, pulling his T-shirt over his head. He slumped into a chair and nodded his thanks at the coffee set before him.

"Should you be up, friend?" Sean slid a plate of food in front of Candace.

"I need to be. I'm feeling more away all the time, and coffee will definitely help." He sniffed at the aroma wafting through the kitchen. "And some of that food will help. I don't think I've eaten in I don't know how long."

"You've been gone for a few days." Sean and Candace shared a look. "Here. Eat this. Then we need to plan."

Jonah picked up his fork and then stared at his plate, a frown on his face.

"It's really good, Jonah." Candace's voice reached him and he dug into the food.

"You haven't lost your touch, Sean. It takes like your Mom's."

"Thanks. She'd be glad to hear that. She was asking about you the other day." Sean stopped, staring at Jonah, a though crossing his mind. "Jonah, who would want to hurt you the most in town?"

Jonah looked up, a thoughtful look on his face. "There are a few that are jealous of how well I'm doing. You don't think they'd go to the point of contaminating my place, do you?"

Candace stared at him, the thought never having crossed her mind. "If that happens, then you lose your organics status, right?"

Jonah nodded. "I would, but I don't think that's what this is all about." He stood, waited to catch his balance, and then began to pace, his hands thrust into his pockets. He finally stopped, wiping a hand through his hair. "I know who it is and I know exactly how to bring them out." He spun to stare at the two sitting at the table. "It's going to take some work, but we should be able to do it."

"All right, then. Let's plan." Sean reached to clear the table as Candace searched for paper and pens.

Two hours later, their plans were made. A call to Andrew filled him in and he promised to bring the three detectives up to date on what the plans were.

"It will take a day or two for word to get back to this person. Then, we can show up and make our move."

Candace sat back, her eyes on the paper she had been taking notes on. "How far does this go, Jonah? How many are involved?"

He shrugged. "We won't know until we actually get the leader." He was frustrated, his body telling him he needed to sleep but he didn't want to.

Sean studied him and then pointed back to the bedroom. "Sleep, Jonah. Let your body heal. We need you as close to normal as we can get to bring this group down.

❦ ❦ ❦ ❦

Two days passed and Jonah finally stood at Sean's car, his eyes searching around. Sean had been right. No one had found them. He turned as he felt a hand on his arm and stared down at Candace. They were ready to put their plan into play. He was worried. These people had shown along that they weren't afraid to hurt anyone.

"Are you ready to do this, Jonah? We can make new plans." She searched his face.

He reached up to cup her cheek. "It's you I'm worried about, love. They may go after you again."

She shook her head. "Not if you're back in the open and we're together. They want you, not me. That's what it's been all along. Everything that happened to me has been to draw you out. They've been

231

watching you for a long time, Jonah, waiting for the right opportunity. And I just happened to have a table beside you that day, that started it all off."

He nodded, his head raising to share a look with Sean. "Let's do this then, if you're sure. You can back out any time."

"We'd never live with ourselves if we back out. We'd never have a life." She slid into the car, and the two men joined her.

Silas turned from the front of the church as he heard the door to the sanctuary open and close and then footsteps approaching him. He studied the two men and women, then sighed. Here we go again, he thought.

"Jonah. Candace. Glad to see you two are all right."

"Thank you, Silas. This is a friend of mine, Sean." Jonah made the introductions, keeping them simple. "Can we talk?"

Silas pointed at the pews and sat in the front one, watching as Jonah sat in the one behind him beside Candace, reaching for her hand. Sean slid into the one behind the couple.

"Now, you wanted to talk. What about?" Silas watched as the three exchanged glances. "It's not that bad, is it?"

Candace shared a look with Jonah, before sneaking a peek at Sean. "It depends on how you view it, Silas. I'll let Jonah explain. You know him better than you do me."

Silas nodded even as he turned to Jonah. When Jonah didn't speak, Silas smiled. "I know you, Jonah. You're not sure about all this, are you? Has it to do with what you two have been through?"

He nodded. "It is." He sighed, then ran his hands through his hair before clasping them behind his neck. "I'm really not sure how to explain what we want to do."

"At the beginning is usually a good place. Let me guess. You two are going to pretend something in order to draw out whoever it is that's after you."

Candace stared at him. "How'd you know that?"

Silas started laughing. "You're not the first of his friends to try something like this.

So, tell me. What is your plan and how do I come into it?"

Jonah spoke rapidly with Candace and Sean adding points where they were needed, Silas asking questions when he needed to clarify something.

Silas finally stood and paced to the back of the sanctuary and back. "It could work, but it might not. It all depends on how well you two act and if your plans will even draw out the leader. Have you talked to Andrew at all about this?"

Jonah shook his head. "He knew we were planning something. We did give him some preliminary ideas, but we've been refining them since we talked to him."

Silas nodded. "I see. This isn't something I can just jump into, you three. I need to pray about it first. If the Lord tells me no, then I can't help you."

"We understand, Silas. Either way, we'd like your prayers and support."

"You have those. Now, come back tomorrow at this time. Give me twenty-four hours to pray it over." He walked away

234

towards his office as the three stood and headed out of the church.

"What do we do if he doesn't help us?" Candace was worried, not sure how long they had before they were attacked again.

"Then we go to Plan B." Sean stated.

Jonah stared at him. "We have a Plan B?"

Sean laughed as he pulled away from the church. "We do. And a plan through every letter of the alphabet, although my hope is that Plan A works."

"Where do we go now?" Candace stared around, sure they had been spotted and someone would catch them right away.

Sean didn't respond, just drove out of town and headed south from where they had been. "I have another place we can stay at. Don't worry, it's not known."

Jonah stood later that afternoon, looking out the kitchen window towards the woods at the back. He didn't feel safe, and he turned to find Candace near him. He reached to draw her over to him, wrapping his arms around her.

"Jonah, I don't like this place. I don't feel safe."

He nodded. "I don't either. Where's Sean?"

"I don't know. He disappeared somewhere a while ago. How much do you trust him?"

Jonah shrugged. "We've been friends for years, but today, I'm not sure of him." He turned to look towards the door. "Listen, I know where we are. We can leave, just the two of us, if that's what you want."

"How?"

Jonah nodded towards the back door. "Out there and into the woods. Come on. Something's telling me we need to move and move now. Grab your backpack and I'll grab some water and food. We need to leave before Sean comes back."

She scurried off and returned with her backpack. Jonah stuffed water and packages of food into it and then grabbed some fruit. He pointed to the door, his finger to his mouth in a quietening motion. She nodded, slipping through the door and to the woods, Jonah on her heels. They had no more reached the woods then heard the sounds of tires on the gravel driveway. Jonah pushed her further into the woods, finding a narrow trail for them to follow.

"What about Sean?" Jonah could barely hear her question.

"Pray he stays safe." Jonah frowned. "There's something I'm missing in all this. Quick, do you have your phone?"

She nodded and reached for a pocket on the backpack. "Here. Who do you need to call?"

"Call Richard. He lives near here. Hopefully he can come and get us. I don't want to go back with Sean."

She nodded even as she spoke with Richard. He assured her that he would be there, waiting for them, once they made it through the woods. A sudden yell stopped them in their tracks. Then, Jonah was pushing at her, making her run.

They broke through the woods and Richard was there, waiting for them. He hustled them into his truck and away. He watched for anyone behind him but didn't see anyone. He drove rapidly through

Elmton and out to the country, to a safe house he had used in the past.

"You can talk to me later. Let me call the county and have them check out that house." He pointed to the house door. "Get yourselves in there, now. Stay away from the windows. If needed, there's a door in the pantry floor, near the back. Go down it and you'll be safe. I'll be in shortly to show you."

Richard pocketed his phone after speaking with the county police. He knew he had to talk to Jonah, but he needed a few minutes to gather his thoughts. Jonah was not going to like what he had found out.

"Richard?" Candace's voice greeted him as he shut and locked the door.

He turned, seeing the concern on her face that changed to understanding. He swung an arm around her shoulder in a hug, then pointed towards the office, where Jonah was working on the computer, trying to find information.

"Come on. I need to talk to both of you." Regret and sorrow shaded his voice.

Jonah turned as he heard Richard's voice. "What did you find out? Richard?"

Richard shook his head as he sat, facing the two of them. "It's not good news, Jonah. Sean is dead, but they found evidence that he was working with the group that was after you."

Jonah stared at him, mouth opening and closing. "He was working with them? Then, why did he do what he did?"

"We don't know that and we may not. The county force did manage to arrest one of the men, and he's talking. But whatever plans you came up with, you can be assured that they were known to the group."

Jonah sat back, his mind whirling. "We need to get to Silas then. He's in danger."

"Already done. I have someone with him."

"Now what, Richard?" Candace finally spoke.

"Now we come up with a plan. We're not sure what all Sean was after, but between the departments, it will be searched out." He looked between the two. "No more running. No more making plans that could get you killed. Understand?"

Candace nodded, her face white with fear. "Richard, we have to do something." Then she groaned. "You didn't talk to Abe, did you?"

"No. Should I have?" He grinned at the glare she shot him. "He's out of town anyway."

"You did try, didn't you?" She walked out of the room, frustration evident.

"You shouldn't have done that, Richard. She's trying to break free of having them in her life like this."

"I know she is, Jonah, but right now, that's what's needed. For you, too." He leaned forward. "Okay, now let's plan. What were you trying to do anyway? Maybe I can come up with a new plan for you."

Jonah looked at him and shook his head, his eyes going towards where he could see Candace. She was standing watching him.

Chapter 19

The news story broke late that afternoon, giving the details of the investigation that Andrew would release, and naming suspects in custody. He was pushing to get this over with.

Jonah and Candace stood in the conference room, surrounded by techs and officers frantically working through the myriad of information and documentation they had amassed.

"Where does it end, Andrew?" Candace's question had him turning back to her.

"This news story will shake them up. We haven't given all the details, just what we needed to. Hopefully, they'll make a move. We have officers at both your places, similar enough to you that until the culprits are up close, they can't tell the difference."

Jonah nodded. "I know but it worries me, Andrew. They're not safe."

"They are well aware of what we're facing, Andrew. Each one volunteered to be the decoy. Leslie's staying out at your place as well, Jonah."

He nodded. "I still don't like it. But where does that leave us? We have to go somewhere."

"The safest place is likely right here. I've had cots put into the boardroom for you both." He held up his hands. "Just for the night for now. We'll reassess it tomorrow." He looked around. "Now, let's get you two in there and then Ev has promised to bring in meals for us all."

Candace threw herself down on her cot, face down. Tears were close and she didn't want Jonah to see. Jonah knew but he pretended he didn't, trying to let Candace have her privacy. A knock came at the door, and then it opened, Bill standing there with containers of food in his hands.

"Here. Ev brought your favourites, I think. Eat up. She said she didn't want to see any left over and she would inspect the garbage to make sure you had eaten everything."

Jonah shook his head as he took the containers. "I'm not sure how much we'll be able to eat. Thanks, Bill."

He turned to Candace. "Come on, love. Let's each something."

Candace sat up, her fatigue evident. "I'm not sure I can eat anything."

"Just try. That's all we ask."

❧ ❧ ❧ ❧

Andrew stood at the open door the next morning, watching the couple. Candace still seemed to be asleep. Jonah was up, his Bible open in front of him. Bill had gone and got it for him the day before.

"Jonah? Can I talk to you a moment?" Andrew kept his voice low.

Jonah nodded, even as he rose to his feet, his eyes on Candace.

"Sure, what about?"

"We've had word that the group is making new plans. They know you spent the night here. It wasn't one of our officers, before you ask. They likely saw you come

243

in and not leave." Andrew paced in the hallway, his mind working through possibilities. "We need to get you two out of here and to safety."

"But where, Andrew? They seem to find us all the time."

Andrew nodded. "I know they do. Let me work something through. Silas called. He had a visitor last night, who seemed interested in what he was doing for you. He didn't confirm or deny anything."

"I don't like that, Andrew. Are our families safe?"

"They are. Your parents wanted to head back this way, but we talked them into staying where they are. Candace's family have gone away, somewhere she won't know where to find them."

"That's good."

"What's good?" Candace spoke from behind him and he spun.

"Our families are safe."

"That is good news. Now what, Andrew? I heard what you and Jonah were talking about."

Andrew nodded. "I leave you here for a while and then move you somewhere."

"I hope you have a good plan to do that. They seem to know exactly where we are all the time."

"I know. We've searched for GPS and tracking devices and found none. Your phones both have the GPS locator turned off. Someone is keeping a close eye on you both."

"Yeah, they are. The last few days it would have been through Sean, but now?"

Andrew nodded, then pointed at the room. "Back in there. I'll be back in a couple of hours."

Jonah paced the room, Candace sitting and watching him.

"Jonah, what can we do?"

He shrugged. "Andrew's trying to come up with a plan."

"I know he is, but I can't just sit here. I need to be doing something."

"I know how you feel." He sat beside her on the cot. "Now, what plans can we come up with?"

She shrugged. "Every time we do, someone finds us."

"Maybe because someone is listening in on us."

He held a finger to his mouth, then pointed at the pad of paper and pen she had been doodling on. He wrote rapidly, she responded, and then they agreed on a plan. She searched through her backpack, pulling out what she needed, and then pointed at the door.

He nodded, moving to leave the room first. He searched for Andrew and not seeing him moving quietly towards the front of the building, finally just walking out. He sat on a bench across the street, watching as Candace slipped out too. Joining hands, they walked rapidly away.

Andrew stood in the room doorway, not seeing them there, then searched the building, knowing that they had made it out and away from them without anyone noticing. He found Bill, who shrugged.

"You know they weren't going to sit still."

"I know. I was hoping they would. Now, we need to find them again."

"They'll find us, Andrew, when they're ready to. They're likely safer out of here."

Andrew nodded. "They may be but they could be more at risk as well. Let the patrol officers know to look for them." He sighed. "Now I have to call Richard and let him know to look for them."

❧ ❧ ❧ ❧

Jonah pulled Candace to a stop and into a doorway. He looked around, not seeing anyone following them at present. He searched her face and then nodded.

"We'll keep going. You're up to it?"

"I am, Jonah. I just hope we're doing the right thing. Are you sure you know who's behind this?"

He nodded. "It's the only person that makes sense. They moved here about fifteen years ago and took over a rundown farm. They've made improvements but there is no way theirs is a true organic farm. I know the farm and the soil. It's too contaminated with chemicals for them to ever get an organics license.”

“So, they bought someone off?”

“More than likely. Come on. It’s not that much further.”

Candace sighed, then followed Jonah as he walked away. He reached for her hand and nestled hers close in his.

An hour later, he stopped and pointed. “There. Silas is home. We’ll wait for a bit to see if anyone’s watching him.”

“And if they are?”

“Then we wait until dark.”

She nodded, exhaustion evident in her movements. Jonah swept her close, holding her upright against him. He looked around for somewhere for her to sit, but didn’t see anything close. His eyes returned to Silas’ home and he finally made a decision. He led her across the road and around to the backyard, seating her in one of the outdoor chairs before moving to the door and quietly knocking.

Silas stood, staring at Jonah and then past him at Candace, before moving aside so they could enter. Jonah swept Candace up in his arms and carried her through to the couch, gently setting her down, before watching her lie down and close her eyes. He reached for the afghan and covered her before turning to Silas.

"Silas."

"Kitchen, Jonah. Coffee, I think, and then we talk."

Jonah nodded, sinking gratefully into a chair. "Thank you, Silas. You've been safe?"

Silas nodded. "I have been, but I've been watched. You picked a good time to come. The car just left. It will be back in about an hour."

Jonah drew a breath of relief. "That's good then. God was watching out for us."

"I would say so, but you should have stayed with Andrew."

Jonah shook his head. "That would only prolong it. We want this over with now."

"And how do you plan on doing that?" Silas set the cup of coffee in front of Jonah, then reached for the tin of cookies, before seating himself.

"We're not quite sure. We have a plan, but we need another day to put it into place."

"And that plan would be?" Silas knew somehow it involved him.

Jonah spoke rapidly, Silas silent as he did so. Jonah stopped, watching his friend's face closely.

"I see. And you think this will draw them out?"

"It will. It means going back to my farm. I don't want it here in town."

"Your farm makes it more difficult to keep you safe."

"But it keeps the people in town safe." Jonah sat back, his eyes on his cup. "There's just no good way to do this, Silas. Andrew says he still needs more information. If we can draw them out and catch them in the act, then he'll have what he wants."

"It's too great a risk for both of you." Silas stood, moving towards his phone as it chimed. He studied the message, then set the phone back down before he turned. "Andrew knows you're here. How?"

Jonah shrugged. "A good guess on his part, I would say. Listen, if you don't want to help, tell me and we'll move on."

Silas held up a hand. "No, I'll help. I just don't have to like it, now do I?"

Jonah stood, his movements slow as fatigue washed through him. He held onto the chair to keep his balance, not seeing Silas move towards him until he touched his arm.

"Come, Jonah. Use the spare room. You've been through a lot in the last few days and you need rest."

Jonah nodded slowly, turning as Silas pointed out the way.

❦ ❦ ❦ ❦

Late that night, Silas stopped his car near Jonah's farm, turning to the couple.

"You wanted me to let you off here. Just know that Leslie's at your house as is an officer."

"We know. I wish I could get them out of there." Jonah was frustrated.

"No. They need to be there. They'll help with your plans. Now before you two leave, let's pray."

Leslie looked up from his paper as Jonah walked into his kitchen, Candace on his heels. He folded it and laid it down.

"Figured you'd be here soon. It's just me here." He rose from the table. "Now that you're back, I'm assuming you have plans."

"We do and we'll need your help. We're planning on flushing them out." Jonah's voice hardened. He had had enough and wanted it over. "I plan on sending them an email early tomorrow morning, stating what I know and where they can find me."

"That's living dangerously, Jonah."

He nodded. "I know it is. I'll need your help, Leslie. Candace has to stay in the house. I don't want her out in the open while this goes down."

"You think they'll come here?"

"I know they will. Andrew's got their group down to just two or three."

Leslie agreed. He had talked to Andrew not that long before Jonah walked in. Andrew had realized what Jonah was planning, just didn't have the timing for it.

"Are you planning on letting Andrew know?"

"I'll give the group a time to be here, and let Andrew know once they've agreed to it. Of course, they won't keep to that time. They'll be early."

"That they will. Just let me know where you want me."

"I think in the far greenhouse. The door opens to the fields. I plan on being out in the open and making them come to me."

"They could put someone in the trees with a long-range rifle, you know."

"Somehow I don't think they will. This is too personal for them now. They want to be close to me for anything to go down." He looked at Candace. "I know you don't like it, Candace, but this is the only way it will work."

She nodded, then headed down the hall and up the stairs to one of the spare rooms. She didn't like what Jonah was planning, but knew it might be the only way to end this.

Jonah watched her walk away, then turned back to Leslie, finalizing plans with him. He finally sought his own bed, laying awake and restless, his mind going over everything before he finally turned to prayer. He wasn't sure if God would be there or prevent anything but he knew he could only trust.

Chapter 20

_Late the next morning, Jonah headed for the fields, taking in all the work Leslie had put in when he was not there. He nodded, his mind not quite on why he was out there. He loved the land and wanted to see it flourish. If this group had their way and got his land, it would be ruined with chemicals.

He knew Leslie was hidden in the greenhouse, the door propped open. Candace had promised to stay inside, the doors locked, and keep away from the windows. Andrew and Bill waited down the road, patrol officers with them. Jonah figured the group would come in from the back of the farm.

He turned as he sensed someone watching him and knew his assessment had been right. The three walked towards him over the ruts in the fields, two men and a women. He could hear faint voices and knew the woman was complaining. It was what she did best, Jonah thought.

They stopped ten feet away from him, staring at him, waiting for him to speak. Instead, he pressed a button on the recorder stuck in his pocket.

"What do you want with us, Jonah? Why bring us out here, into all this dirt?" The women, Madge Simmons, finally spoke. "Is this a joke of some kind?"

"No joke, Madge. You know exactly why you're out here."

She shook her head. "Refresh my memory."

Jonah shook his head. "Doesn't work that way, Madge. I would suggest you talk instead."

"What? You're not talking? That would be a first." He could hear the anger building in her voice. "So what do you want to talk about? The organics farm you have here? I bet you're not making the money that I am."

Jonah held up the papers he had been holding in his left hand. "Here's your profits, Madge.   Public record and all. There have been more inspections on your farm.   Funny thing.   You have to have inspections all the time to continue to be certified as an organics farmer.   I've obtained the last couple of yours.   Not certified as organics.   You're using chemicals."

She strode towards him, stumbling some on the clods of dirt. "Give me that." She reached to tear the paperwork from him, but he tucked it away inside his shirt.

"Even if you took this, the authorities have copies. They were very interested in what you've been doing."

Her face hardened and twisted. "You've ruined it all. We had a good thing going until you hooked up with that woman. You never looked into anything. We tried to warn her off and warn you off but it didn't work."   She beckoned to the two men. "Finish him off.   Make it look like an accident of some kind."

Jonah stood tall even as the men stepped towards him. They didn't see the officers approaching from behind them or Leslie coming from the greenhouse.

"It's over, Madge. These officers are here to place you all under arrest. They know exactly what you've one over the past weeks, the body in Candace's freezer, the bloody knife, the text messages, the letters, the kidnappings, the assaults."

"I'm not falling for that, Jonah. There's no one here but us."

"And that is where you would be wrong." Andrew's voice had her spinning and struggling to keep her balance in the rutted fields. "You're all under arrest. This time, Madge, you won't get away. I understand other jurisdictions are looking for you and your henchmen."

She tried to stare down Andrew as cuffs were closed around her wrists. "I'll have your job for this."

Andrew gave a small smile. "I don't think so. We've got all the evidence we need. And when we're done, you'll be moved on to the next city. Enjoy your last bit of fresh air and freedom. You're looking at a long time behind bars, seeing as it's not just one murder your connected to."

Jonah turned as he heard running footsteps behind him and caught Candace as she threw herself into his arms. He wrapped her close and his head dropped to hers. Andrew watched for a moment, then spoke.

"How be we get you two out of here?" He pointed towards the house. "As in undercover?"

"It's over, isn't it?" Candace raised her head to look at Andrew.

"It is. We just have to ensure we have all the players. I think we do but until we're sure, you two stay out of sight. Jonah, it was a foolish thing you did today, but it ended it for you."

"There was no other way, Andrew. If I hadn't, it would have gone on for too long. I was ready for it to end and so was Candace."

❧ ❧ ❧ ❧

A week later, Candace looked up from her desk in her business as Jonah appeared. She rose to be wrapped in his arms and held tight.

"Jonah? Why are you here in the middle of the day?"

"I just had to come and see my girl. I talked to Andrew. Madge finally broke down and confessed. She was altering her records and using produce purchased from my stand to fake the organics reports. She was making a lot of money doing this. She had an inspector on her payroll. She admitted to having us assaulted and kidnapped, although her reasons as so muddled I don't think they'll ever be clear as to why. She did have Sean killed, but he was working with her as well."

"Sean was? I know he was your friend, but there was just something off about him."

Jonah nodded. "I know. I wish he hadn't gotten mixed up with her. His statement that he was investigating organic farmers really didn't make a whole lot of sense."

"What about the others?"

"They're talking as well, to try and get lighter sentences. No matter what happens with them, we've done our part and helped clean up a section of our town. Now, my dear, when you're through, I would like to take you out to dinner." He reached back to the chair beside the door. "These are for you." He handed her a bouquet of red roses.

"Oh, how lovely, Jonah. Thank you." She reached to hug him. "I'm about through for the day, anyway. Is it a dress-up dinner or just casual?"

"Dress up, please. I have."

She noticed for the first time that he was in a suit and tie. "I never noticed. Follow me home or give me thirty minutes and I'll be ready."

"Take as long as you like, my dear. You're worth the wait."

She looked up, saw the look in his eyes, and blushed, her face going back to her roses. She couldn't speak. What they were feeling was too young and fresh for words, even if it did make her feel like a teenager again.

Epilogue

*J*onah studied the twinkling lights he had hung around his back deck and then turned as he heard the door open behind him. It was a cooler night, but he didn't care. The woman he loved was standing here, her mouth slightly open, as she stared around.

"Jonah? What's going on?"

He grinned and reached for her. "Just an ordinary dinner, love."

She shook her head. "No, it's not. You're up to something."

He reached for her hand, drawing her out onto the deck. "I really do have a dinner planned for you. Let's get you seated."

He pushed her chair in for her and then headed for the kitchen, returning with their dinner. Talk was casual, they had spent enough time together to know what the other was thinking. Jonah watched the contentment and peace on her face and thanked God that she was in his life. He reached for her hand, drawing her to her feet and walked down the yard with her, Rusty running around them.

"Jonah. Thank you for dinner. It was delicious."

"You're welcome, love." He stopped, turning her to face him and then suddenly short of words.

Her head tilted towards him, Candace watched and waited for him to speak. "Jonah?"

He bit his lip as he studied her face and finally sighed. "I had the words I wanted to say all memorized but they've just disappeared. So here goes. Candace, you've become the most important thing in my life, right up there after God. Would you be mine for life, grow old with me? Will you marry me?"

She stared at him. She had suspected he was planning on asking her at some point, but not just yet. She finally nodded, unable to find the words.

He reached to kiss her and then drew her close to him. "Thank you, love. I really do love you more than anything here on earth."

She nodded, her hair brushing against his face. "You have my love as well, Jonah." She stood for a moment before pushing back. "But you do understand I come with baggage?"

"Baggage? But don't we all?"

She shook her head even as she laughed. "You know my baggage. Those eight men who like to meddle."

Jonah broke out into laughter. "Oh yes, that baggage. But I think you'll find they won't be meddling any more. I had a talk with each one of them."

"You didn't!" She searched his face. "You did! Thank you."

She stood, her eyes searching his farm. "We'll have a good life here, Jonah, as God wills."

"That we will. With all that we've gone through, our love is strong and sure. God placed each one of us in the other's life. He had a plan and purpose for us. And I hope you never ever doubt the love He has for you."

"There were many times that I did, but you have shown me that God really does love me and wants the best for me. Right now, that includes you. And those plans we made to draw them out by posing as a couple really did come true."

Jonah nodded as he turned them back towards the house, Rusty as close to Candace as he could get. "We need to make plans, love."

"That we do." She stopped for a moment. "We have the rest of our lives to make and keep our plans."

Dear Readers

Thank you for choosing to read the story of Jonah and Candace. It was fun to write and even more fun to have her cousins with Emma from Riverville. The stories of these eight men are found in the *His Guardians* series. Organic farming is becoming more and more a way of life for us. I admire those who dedicate their lives to producing pure products.

There is a segment of our population no matter if you live in the United States or Canada as I do that struggle for meals, for whatever reason. Having Candace take on this task was a shout-out to those involved in this.

God's love is there for us everywhere we turn, no matter what we're facing. He shows us in so many ways.

God bless each one of you.

Ronna